"Reilly, kiss m[...]

"I don't think that'[...]

The rejection stung [...] stop the need. "Kiss me."

"Carey," he protested, only halfheartedly.

"One kiss. One innocent kiss. It's been so long, and I…"

"You what?" he asked, his eyes searching her face.

Wanted him. Couldn't pretend otherwise. "Need you to kiss me."

His eyes darkened and when he surrendered, his mouth capturing hers, the kiss was anything but innocent.

He tried to pull his lips away, perhaps to apologize, but she clamped her hand around the back of his head, holding him to her.

He tasted like mint and he smelled spicy, like a man, a real man.

He finally tore his mouth away. "We can't do this."

Still reeling from the impact of his kiss, she blinked in confusion. "Why? Why can't we?"

"This isn't right. You're the witness in a case."

Dear Reader,

Hiding His Witness is my first book with Harlequin Romantic Suspense. I'm a longtime reader and fan of the line and am thrilled to be published alongside some of my favorite authors.

The Truman brothers are loosely based on my brothers—three strong men who are always competing with each other and involved in some good-natured ribbing. When push comes to shove, they circle the wagons, a favorite phrase of my father's, and have each other's backs. Who wouldn't want a family like that?

The heroine, Carey, has the opposite family life. She has no one to rely on and is constantly looking over her shoulder.

It was fascinating for me to write about two very different characters and the situation that brings them together. I hope you enjoy reading this book as much as I enjoyed writing it.

Happy reading!

C.J. Miller

C.J.
MILLER

Hiding His Witness

HARLEQUIN®
entertain, enrich, inspire™

Recycling programs
for this product may
not exist in your area.

ISBN-13: 978-0-373-27792-6

HIDING HIS WITNESS

C.J. MILLER

is a third-generation Harlequin reader and the first in her family to write professionally. She lives in Maryland with her husband and young son. She enjoys spending time with family, meeting friends for coffee, reading and traveling to warm beaches around the world. C.J. believes in first loves, second chances and happily ever after.

C.J. loves to hear from readers and can be contacted through her website at www.cj-miller.com.

To Brook, for always reading and believing.

Chapter 1

After the streetlights came on, traveling alone along the empty sidewalk was a very bad idea. But Carey didn't have money for a cab and the bus didn't run at this late hour. She had no choice but to walk home. Most of the time she didn't mind being one of the nameless, faceless inhabitants of the city. City meant anonymity, avoiding eye contact, and a life so fast-paced most people didn't remember her name or when and where she moved.

And Carey moved quite frequently.

What she did mind were the rotten jobs she'd had to work the last eleven months. Without a social security card—or at least not one she was willing to share with her employers—the jobs were monotonous, low paying, and the hours terrible, hence her walk alone in the dark at midnight.

Carey pulled her jacket tighter around her, staving

off the cold and clutching her *Vogue* magazine to her chest, and looked over her shoulder, left then right. With the news media blasting details of the grisly serial killings committed in this neighborhood, she prayed with every step she'd make it home safely.

She kept the hood of her worn gray sweatshirt tugged over her head, her baggy clothes disguising her gender, and stepped up her pace. Steam poured from the grates along the sidewalk and the streetlights that weren't broken illuminated her way. Her landmark was the twenty-four-hour convenience store located across from her apartment building, its bright white lights and red-and-green sign shining into her windows. Three more blocks.

In the distance, police sirens wailed, sending a shiver up her spine. Another mugging? A murder?

"Shut up. I told you to shut up," a voice bit into the night.

Carey froze, her muscles tightening, every instinct she had going on the alert.

Grunts and the dull thud of fists on flesh escaped from the alleyway ahead. Kicking into survival mode, she reached into her oversize jeans and grabbed her pepper spray, flattening herself against the brick building at the corner of the alley. Her heart hammered against her rib cage, threatening to reveal her presence. What should she do? Scramble into the entryway of the building and hope she went unnoticed? Turn and run in the other direction? Call for help? She didn't have a cell phone and pay phones had long since disappeared from the street. If she knocked on any of the doors along this row, would anyone answer?

Probably not. This late at night, a knock on the door brought trouble.

Peering into the alley, she made out the shadow of a man, the glint of his knife blade catching in the street-light. A drug deal gone bad? Had she stumbled on a mugging? The man with the knife shifted, bringing into view another man cringing on the ground against the wall, his arm shielding his face.

Her father used to tell her there came a moment in every person's life where courage was tested. Fight or flight.

Rage charged in her veins. Fight. Definitely fight.

Screaming, "Fire! Fire!" at the top of her lungs, hoping the word brought attention to the alley, Carey bowled herself into the attacker, blasting her pepper spray in his face. The liquid caught on her finger and burned like fire. A hit to the eyes had to be worse.

The man swore at her, stumbled backward, and slammed her into the wall behind them. Her spine hit the brick with a hard crack, absorbing the impact, making her teeth clatter. She hadn't quite gathered her wits when the assailant grabbed her shoulders, throwing her to the ground like a rag doll. Her head banged into the cement, jarring her vision. The attacker wiped at his eyes, swearing every curse word she'd ever heard, swinging the knife in his hand wildly.

His face was one she would never, ever forget. Dark hair, beady eyes, a hawklike nose and thin lips. Launching himself at her, he slashed his knife through the air, and she rolled, almost managing to avoid the blade. She ignored the sharp sting on her arm as his knife brushed past her. Letting out a bellow of anger, he kicked at her, missing once. He kicked again, connecting with her rib cage.

Curling to protect her head from his blows, she tried to scramble away from him, still shouting, "Fire! Fire!"

She'd been on the run for nearly a year and she wasn't about to die in a cold, dark alley at the hands of a knife-wielding thug.

A police siren howled closer, and with a final litany of curses aimed at her, her attacker took off in the opposite direction, barreling through a line of trash cans and disappearing into the night.

Carey groaned as she moved onto her hands and knees, her body battered, her left arm stinging. She set her hand over the cut and pressed down, hoping it wasn't too deep and wouldn't need stitches. Dragging herself to her feet, she limped toward the man slumped against the wall, unmoving. She touched her fingers to his neck, looking for a pulse. Her hands shook so violently, she couldn't tell if he was dead or alive. She had to get him help.

A woozy feeling passed over her and she fought for focus and control. If she lost consciousness, there was no telling where she would end up. Taking several deep breaths, she moved toward the opening to the alley. Leaning against the corner of the building, hand still pressed over her arm, she cried out again.

Mercifully, the flash of red-and-blue drew closer and an unmarked car with a dash light drew to a hard stop less than fifty feet from her.

Two men leapt from the car, drawing their weapons. "Police. Get your hands in the air."

They weren't in uniform and she quashed the impulse to run. Could she trust they were who they claimed? How could she be sure they weren't dirty and corrupt?

Making a quick decision to believe them, at least for now, she held up her hands obediently, wincing as her arm and ribs cried out in protest. "Don't shoot. There's a man in the alley. He needs an ambulance." She pointed behind her with her left index finger, keeping her hands in the air.

One of men raced into the alley and the second holstered his gun, rushing to her. She let her hands drop, the pain in her left arm unbearable.

He towered over her, close enough to touch her, close enough for her to feel the heat radiating from his body. His eyes raked over her and she could scarcely draw a full breath under his scrutiny, her rib cage aching with every inhale, her heart skittering frantically. Fear clashed with her desire for comfort and the sudden urge to lean into him. She was losing it. She must be losing it if she was thinking about turning to this stranger for help of any kind.

He had the slightly dangerous look of man who was a little bit reckless and lived life on his own terms. His hair was dark, worn longer than most men, and a shadow of a beard covered his jawline. With broad shoulders and slim hips, he captured her interest and that was troubling. She didn't have the time or energy to be interested in anyone.

"Are you hurt?" he asked, his dark eyes singeing her with concern.

Carey shook her head, the lie a necessary one. The fierce cold bit into her hands, her chin stung and her arm throbbed. She turned to keep him from seeing her injury. Panic swept over her. She had to get out of here. She couldn't stay a moment longer. She'd clean and bandage her arm herself later. The convenience store sold bandages, didn't they? "I'm fine."

He narrowed his gaze on her as if he didn't believe her. "What happened?"

"I wasn't involved. I just screamed for help."

"I need you to come with me to the station."

Her terror grew stronger. She needed a plan of escape. She couldn't go with him to the police station. He couldn't force her, could he? "I just want to go home." Black spots dotted her vision. She needed to lie down. Soon.

He shook his head and a lock of hair fell over his forehead. "I need to take your information and a statement about what happened here."

Her gaze drifted to that lock of hair, then to his eyes. Surprised by the smoldering heat she found in them, she felt the look as if he'd touched her. A warm shiver moved down her spine and her stomach tightened. This guy had charisma and raw, sexual magnetism in spades. A man with whom she wouldn't—couldn't—lower her boundaries even a fraction of an inch for fear he'd get inside.

Another siren drew closer and an ambulance turned onto the street. Carey said a mental thank-you for the quick response time and hoped the man in the alley would be okay. She needed to beat feet.

"I didn't see anything." The lie made her ears burn. She could see in his face he didn't believe her.

"You saw enough to call for help."

Why had she stopped and interfered? Why hadn't she kept her head down and kept walking? "I don't remember." What a terrible excuse. Dizziness swept over her and she struggled to remain standing. Home was three blocks away. She could make it.

"Do you have ID?" he asked.

"Do you?"

He lifted a brow, never taking his eyes off her, then reached into his back pocket and drew out his badge.

"May I?" she asked, extending her right hand.

Shooting her a wary look, he handed over his badge for inspection. She opened the wallet, his ID tucked inside. He wasn't a plainclothes police officer—he was a detective. He didn't look older than thirty-five. Impressive that he'd made the ranks that young. Assuming he wasn't dirty, her respect for him ratcheted up a notch. "Detective Reilly Truman. I'm sorry, Detective, but I've got to go." Carey threw the badge behind her for all she was worth and took off in the other direction. She made it two steps and then collapsed, a black hole closing off her thoughts.

Reilly watched his badge sail over her shoulder. He swore under his breath, but his irritation was doused when the witness crumpled to the ground. A moment later he was at her side, rolling her onto her back and checking for a pulse.

She'd passed out beneath a streetlight, giving him a better look at her. Reilly brushed the hair off her face, looking for injuries. Except for the unnatural red color of her hair, her beauty was enthralling, her features small and delicate, and her clothes much too big for her petite frame, as if she were trying to hide her figure. Women this beautiful didn't normally go out of their way to conceal their good looks.

He continued his assessment: a scrape on her chin, a cut on her forehead near her hairline, and her left sleeve was covered in blood. Uneasiness flooded through him. The victim's? Or hers?

The emergency response team converged on the scene, three men treating the victim in the alley, one EMT waiting by the ambulance.

"I need some help," Reilly called over his shoulder.

Pulling away the fabric of her sweatshirt, he saw a cut ran in a narrow slice across her upper arm. It was a recent injury and still bleeding. The urge to help her, the need to make her better, torpedoed through him, as strong as it was unexpected. He never behaved this way on a scene. Reilly was known for keeping his cool, yet his fleeing witness was making him lose it.

The EMT jogged over, kneeling down on the other side of her, spreading open his orange bag. The name "Lou" was stitched on his jacket. "What happened?"

"She passed out. Her arm is bleeding."

Lou pulled on a pair of gloves and Reilly tore away the sleeve of her ratty sweatshirt. The sweatshirt was speckled with pieces of asphalt and the sleeve brushed with red. Her arm was thin, free of track marks or bruises. She didn't have the look or smell of a homeless person. What was she doing on the street at this hour?

Lou examined the wound. "Nasty scratch. Maybe a knife?"

"Could be," Reilly said. Why had she lied when he'd asked if she was hurt? Her serene face was such a contrast to the grit and attitude he'd seen a few minutes before. Reilly took another long look. Yeah, she was pretty all right. Good-looking in a way that would drive a man crazy to kiss her, touch her. In other words, Reilly needed to keep his distance times ten and remember the bad things that could happen when a detective overstepped his bounds. His former partner had taught him that.

Tearing open a packet of alcohol swabs, Lou cleaned her wound and then applied pressure to her sternum with his knuckles to elicit a response. Her cobalt eyes fluttered open then clouded with confusion.

"Hey there, stay with us this time," Reilly said, trying to orient her. He set his hand on her right arm.

She spoke not a word and a moment later, she was kicking and fighting like a wildcat. Reilly held her shoulder and hip to the ground, pinning her body before she kicked him or Lou somewhere sensitive.

"Hey! Calm down. We're helping you," Reilly said.

"No, let go!" She bucked her hips in the air and tried to twist her arms free.

Did he need to call someone in for a psych evaluation? Why were the most attractive ones the most trouble? His breath clouded in the cold night air. "You need medical attention."

"No, I don't," she said through clenched teeth. She stopped fighting him and instead glowered at him as if he was her worst enemy. Spunk; he liked that in a woman. Another time, another place, Reilly would find her tremendously appealing. But today, she was part of an investigation, one that required his full attention.

The air between them vibrated with tension. Reilly forced his focus on the case. "This is Lou. He's an EMT. He's going to fix your arm."

He could see her working the information over in her mind. "Fine," she replied through gritted teeth. She turned her head toward Lou. "Thank you."

The polite words were out of place with the rest of her behavior. But Reilly was on the tail end of a thirty-hour shift, his last before a two-week vacation, and he was in no frame of mind to diagnose the mood swings of a temperamental, yet very pretty, witness.

"Are you hurt anywhere else?" Lou asked her as he cleaned and bandaged her arm.

"I'm fine," she said.

Same lie she'd told him. What was her opposition to medical treatment? Reilly wouldn't let her go home without being sure her injuries had been taken care of and she wouldn't pass out again.

Lou lifted her chin with his fingertips. "You've got some abrasions on your face."

She didn't reply, but flinched when Lou dabbed her chin with another swab. He pressed his hand along her torso. "Does that hurt?"

"No," she said, though tears sprang to her eyes.

If she was hurt, why not say so? The less she said the more Reilly wanted to know about her. He cursed his inquisitive nature and checked his interest. Witness. Firm boundaries.

"Do you think you can stand?" Lou asked. "I'll get the stretcher if you can't. We need to take you to the hospital to get checked out."

The flash of indignation in her eyes told Reilly she would never allow that. "I can manage without the stretcher, and I'm not going to the hospital."

She got to her feet, Lou on one side, him on the other. He wrapped his arm around her slender waist and every muscle in his body flexed in awareness. He ignored the heated rush of sensation. Thin women weren't usually his thing, but as much as he tried to shut it down, an invisible force attracted him to her.

"Are you okay? Dizzy? Woozy?" Lou asked.

"I'm fine. I don't need help."

Reilly was tired of her saying that. She was not fine and he wanted to know why she was lying. If she was in trouble, he could help her.

"Can you tell me your name?" Lou asked.

She ignored him.

"Ma'am, you need to tell us your name," Reilly said, realizing he personally wanted a name to put with this woman even more than he'd need one for his report.

"I don't have one," she said.

"Maybe she has a concussion. You really should

allow us to take you to the hospital. You need a CT scan," Lou said, furrowing his brow, stepping closer and pulling a penlight out of his pocket to check her pupils.

Reilly's police instincts—which were never wrong—told him she was lying. What was she hiding? "She doesn't have a concussion. And if she refuses medical treatment and doesn't tell us her name, then we're going to go down to the precinct and talk that over. Maybe a night in the county jail will refresh her memory." An empty threat. He wouldn't put this woman in lockup. He just wanted her to come clean.

The woman sighed and leveled a look at him. "My name is Carey."

Another lie. He could see it in her eyes. "Okay, Carey. Do you have a last name?"

"Smith."

He'd give her credit for boldness. She didn't even pretend she was being honest.

"And what is your address, Ms. Smith?"

"I don't have one," she said.

Lou smirked.

Reilly maneuvered to stand in front of her, keeping his hands on her waist. She didn't appear quite steady on her feet and he didn't want her passing out again and injuring herself further. "The way you're behaving, you're making me think you did something wrong."

She lifted her scraped chin proudly, meeting his gaze dead-on. "I did nothing wrong. Wrong place, wrong time. I was walking home. I stumbled on something. That's all I know."

Reilly jerked his head, indicating Lou should take off. The witness might be more forthcoming with less of an audience. Lou shrugged, quiet laughter in his eyes, and trotted toward the ambulance, looking over his shoulder once at them.

Yeah, she was a riot.

Carey knew something and she was going to tell him what it was. Reilly closed in on her space, knowing crowding her might pressure the truth from her. "So that's it? Just walking by?" He barely kept the disbelief from his voice, letting her know he was aware she was lying.

"Is the man in the alley okay?" Carey asked, pushing his hands away from her and stepping back.

His palms itched to touch her again. He wasn't giving her another chance to run. He stepped closer. She hadn't answered his question. "Not sure."

She shifted on her feet. "Can you ask someone?"

"We can exchange all the information you want. But I tell you something, you tell me something."

She glared him and pressed her lips together.

Even when she was being difficult, she appealed to him on some primal level. Best to quash those feelings, especially when he was on the job. He had to treat her like any other witness. If she didn't want to talk here, they could talk at the precinct. "Have it your way. I'm hauling you in for questioning."

Sitting alone in the Denver police station in Detective Truman's office, Carey fought the bile that roiled in her stomach. She wished she'd accepted the cola drink he'd offered when they'd first arrived. The bubbles would have settled her stomach, and the caffeine and sugar would have jump-started her brain and helped her think.

She was cold, hungry and tired.

Detective Truman hadn't tossed her into the interrogation room, a small consolation. Instead, she was sitting on a metal chair, amidst his stacks of paper-work and disorganized clutter, waiting for him to return. He'd lobbed a million questions at her, then he'd been interrupted by a phone call and needed to leave for a few minutes. They were the first moments of peace and quiet she'd had to clear her head since stumbling out of that alley.

She tucked her hands into the sleeves of the sweat-shirt Detective Truman had given her since her own had been torn. Unfortunately, this one had DPD across the front. She'd have to ditch it and get another non-descript one later.

Her arm throbbed, but at least it had been cleaned, butterfly stitched and bandaged better than she could have managed on her own.

She closed her eyes, wishing she could lie down for a few minutes. A fifteen-minute nap would revive her and help her sort her thoughts. How could she convince him to let her leave? If she pretended to be insane and babble incoherently, he might set her up with a psych evaluation. Same for pitching a fit and demanding to be allowed to go home. No, she needed a ploy that didn't get her into more trouble.

She scanned the room, looking for clues about his personality, something she could use to play to his sym-pathies. He had no personal items filling the space, no pictures of a wife and children or college degrees mounted to the wall. It looked as though the place hadn't been dusted in a decade and the trash can was filled with empty energy drink cans.

What was the fastest way to get out of this situation? Flirt with him? Lie to him? Tell him what he wanted to hear?

In her former life, flirting with him would have come

easy, letting the fluttering feeling in her stomach dictate her actions. She wasn't that woman anymore. Carey didn't allow herself to get involved with anyone, much less a handsome detective who could undo the hard work she'd put into keeping herself hidden.

If she wasn't running, running, always running, she'd allow herself to daydream about Detective Truman. But daydreaming led to distractions and distractions left her vulnerable.

Staying focused and alert had kept her alive for eleven months and she wasn't about to let down her guard with anyone. She had a long list of precautions—looking behind her on her way to and from work, leaving flour at her front door entrance so she'd know if someone had been inside and never sharing personal information about her life, past or present. She couldn't trust anyone. People could be bought. Information could be sold. And if she befriended an honest person, they might end up getting hurt. Or worse. She didn't want that responsibility.

She begrudgingly admitted Detective Truman wasn't *pure* evil. After securing her in the back of his unmarked squad car, he'd taken control of the scene, giving orders and direction. For nearly two hours, she'd watched him with rapt fascination, the way he moved, the way he spoke. The medics, EMTs and other officers on the scene had looked at him with respect and listened to him out of deference, not fear.

He was confident and sure of himself. She was lonely and he made her feel protected. It was an unsafe combination.

Detective Truman had a disarming quality about him, a "come confide in me" face, and a strong, yet gentle nature. He didn't slam her around or handle her roughly getting her in and out of the car. Giving her the sweatshirt and offering something to drink was nice, but she wouldn't let that break down her defenses.

If she felt anything, it was the basic need for companionship, the loneliness festering in her chest that craved human contact and conversation. She didn't own a phone and no one bothered to check on her in her apartment. How long had it been since someone asked how she was doing and truly cared to hear the answer?

She shook her head, throwing the brakes on that train of thought. She had more important things to think about. Like how she was going to get out of this situation.

Detective Reilly entered his office, closing the door behind him with a soft snick. He'd unbuttoned the sleeves of his dress shirt and rolled them to the elbow. It made for a casual, stylish look. She doubted he'd been going for that. He didn't seem like the type to worry about fashion. Then again, she didn't know anything about him except that he was a detective. She'd be smart to remember that.

Should she ask for a lawyer? Was this the scene where he played good cop with her, giving her a chance to come clean before he and his partner shook her down? Maybe she'd been watching too many crime dramas on television, but without a social life to speak of, her nights were spent alone with the paperbacks she bought for a quarter at the secondhand store or the shows she managed to watch on the old ten-inch television with rabbit ears and a converter she'd salvaged from the Dumpster.

"Just you again?" she asked.

He rubbed his hand across his stubbly jaw. "Would you prefer an audience?"

His sarcasm made her lips nearly twitch into a smile. Laughter. Smiling. She missed those things, too. She forced her face to remain stoic. The important part was never getting emotionally involved. "I need to go home."

"You can go home. I'll take you myself right after we talk. Just tell me your address."

Carey clamped her mouth shut. If she lied, he might try to verify her address before releasing her. And she couldn't tell him the truth. She didn't want her information to go on record and create another thread for Mark to find her. Mark didn't forget about ugly, unfinished business, and he definitely considered her ugly, unfinished business.

Detective Reilly sat down at his desk. "Ms. Smith, may I call you Carey?

Her first name wasn't Carey and her last name wasn't Smith. She didn't care what he called her. None of the last seven aliases she had used for seven different jobs in seven different cities meant anything.

Detective Truman folded his hands and leaned forward. "Ms. Smith, at this time we're not holding you as a suspect."

Magic words. She stood. "I know my rights. I'm leaving."

The warning look on his face froze her in place. "I said, at this time. If you want to change that, I can make arrangements for charges to be brought against you."

Outrage flared in her gut. "I did nothing wrong." Being a Good Samaritan had been a mistake. While she was glad to know that her humanity and compassion hadn't been stripped away by the last eleven months, it had been a mistake to get involved.

"The man in the alley was stabbed in the chest." He spoke with clinical detachment, no hint of emotion.

Carey's stomach twisted. "Is he going to be okay?" An image of the attacker flashed in her mind's eye and she shuddered, a chill running along her spine. She'd see his face every time she closed her eyes for months. Just what she needed—another living nightmare.

Detective Truman stood and circled the desk, leaning his hip on the edge, staring directly at her. A nonthreatening posture, but one that showed interest, closing in on her. Nice psych trick. But she knew those little mind games. She'd played some of them. She wouldn't believe Detective Truman gave a rat's tail about her as anything but a witness.

"The victim's in critical condition at St. Luke's Medical Center. It's important you share everything you remember."

"I didn't see anything," she said, feeling as though she'd spoken those words a hundred times in the past few hours. She'd told Reilly the same thing at the scene and again on the drive to the police station.

He ignored her and pressed on. "The M.O. matches the pattern of several other cases we're working."

A tremor of fear coursed over her and the hairs on the back of her neck stood on end. "What other cases?"

"I'm not permitted to discuss specifics at this time," he said, his eyes holding a cold, distant expression.

Pieces and clips fell into place in a rush. The news programs warning the city. The knife and the alley. The time of night. He was talking about the case that had captured the attention of the police force, the mayor and the entire city. She had trouble taking a full breath as the impact of the realization socked her in the gut. "You're talking about the Vagabond Killer. You think I fought the Vagabond Killer."

Chapter 2

The Vagabond Killer had held the city of Denver and the surrounding towns in his grip of terror for months. No one had survived his attacks and no witnesses had come forward. People traveled in groups or stayed off the streets when they could, especially at night, his preferred time to attack.

Carey struggled for composure. If the attacker in the alley was the Vagabond Killer, was she in danger? Had he seen her face? She'd blasted him point-blank with pepper spray, but she wasn't certain how long it impaired someone's vision.

"At this time, we haven't determined if the cases are related," Detective Truman said.

Carey absently rubbed her finger over the bandage on her arm. If the Vagabond Killer had seen her, she was as good as dead. Staying off the grid was a struggle before the incident in the alley. Now she had two killers after her. She fought the urge to either laugh or cry, to release some of the terror mounting in her chest.

"You saw his face," Detective Truman said. It wasn't a question or an accusation. He spoke it as fact.

"I, um, I sprayed him with pepper spray." She didn't want to admit she'd seen his face. If it leaked to the media that a witness had survived and could identify him, it was the same as painting a bull's-eye over her heart. "Did the man in the alley see him?"

"We don't know. He isn't up to talking. Why were you there?"

She shouldn't answer his questions. Her sleep-deprived mind was only half functioning. She'd already revealed too much, and if she wasn't careful, she would make a mistake and give him some way to identify her. "I don't know." It was a dunce answer, but the best she could come up with under the increasing haze of exhaustion and fear that clouded her mind.

An amused look crossed his face. "You don't know? Maybe you have memory loss from your injuries and we should take you to the nearest hospital."

Her chin shot up. She wasn't going to the hospital. She was fine, and even if she wasn't, she didn't have valid identification or medical insurance. Those places asked too many questions and maybe someone would figure out who she was. If he was trying to mess with her emotions and throw her off kilter, he was doing a good job.

She mustered her courage and squared her shoulders. She was too smart to fall for his games. "I was walking home from work." *Keep the story simple. Don't give away too much.*

He loosened his tie and unfastened the top button of his shirt. "Where do you work?"

No record of her working at Tidy Joe's would exist. She was paid under the table, in cash, and her boss would deny she worked for him. He didn't want trouble from the Department of Labor. The answers to Detective Truman's questions sank her deeper into trouble. Silence was best.

Detective Truman set his hand on her shoulder and her body temperature elevated. "Look, Carey. I can help you. But you have to level with me."

His hand felt heavy on her shoulder, comforting in an odd way. The man was built like a solid rock, with intelligent, knowing eyes. Carey stared at him, weighing her options. The compulsion to tell him the truth was strong, but at the same time alarm bells shrieked in her mind. What was it about him that made her want to give away too much? She wouldn't be taken in by a handsome man. This wasn't about the Vagabond Killer or how much she was drawn to Detective Truman. This was about her personal safety.

He let his hand drop and she muffled a protest. She was clearly starved for affection when she craved a hand on her shoulder. It was the most physical human contact she'd had in months. Well, besides the Vagabond Killer tossing her around that alley, and that wasn't anything to take comfort in.

She wrapped her arms around her stomach. She knew he wasn't letting her leave until she told her side of the story. What difference did it make if she told him the truth now? She had to get out of Denver anyway. Once she was released, she'd go home, grab the emergency bag she kept locked in her closet, and be outside the city limits before the sun set on another day.

The fastest way out was the truth. "I work for Tidy Joe's, the Laundromat about ten blocks from the alley."

She looked up at him to gauge his reaction. He had folded his hands on his knee and his face was consumed with interest, as if what she was telling him was the most fascinating information he'd heard that day. "I was walking home from work and I heard a noise. When I saw what was going on, I ran into the alley and sprayed the guy in the face." It had happened fast and the exact sequence was blurred in her mind. "He tossed me around and I fought back. He ran when he heard the police sirens."

"Tossed you around?"

Was it concern in his eyes? No, she wouldn't believe it. "He cut my arm and I hit my head on the pavement." Among other things. But if Detective Truman used medical attention as an excuse to delay her, the situation grew riskier. She had to make tracks.

Detective Truman stood and walked behind her. "Show me."

In the short time she'd known him, she'd learned he didn't give up. The man was relentless when he wanted something. Carey pushed back the hood of the DPD sweatshirt and touched her head, wincing at the sting. She couldn't see the damage, but the pain told her it wasn't good.

His fingers brushed her hair away from the injury. "Why didn't you have the EMT treat you?" His voice was less stern than it had been a few minutes before.

"I forgot about my head," she muttered. The burn in her arm and ribs had taken precedence over what she was sure would be classified as a nasty bump.

"Wait here," he grumbled and left the room, returning with a first aid kit and a glass of water. He held up a packet of alcohol wipes. "May I?"

She nodded. It would save time to get it cleaned now.

Who knew when she'd next find a safe place to rest or get medical supplies? "I could use some aspirin if you have it." *And a cup of coffee. And a hot meal.* How long had it been since she last ate?

Reilly dug through the kit and tossed a sealed package of generic aspirin on the table.

"Could you open that for me? I'm a little shaky," she said. Suddenly hyperaware of fingerprints, she took precaution not to touch anything. She didn't think her prints would be in the police computer system, but she couldn't be sure. Mark could have taken her prints from anything in the house and paid someone to put her in the system, falsely flagging her as a wanted criminal. He'd go that far to find her. How sophisticated and centralized were police computer systems?

Reilly dumped the two white pills on her open palm. Carey tossed them into her mouth, the bitter taste curling her tongue. She gripped the glass, the sleeves of the sweatshirt pulled over her hands, and washed the pills down, pouring the water into her mouth, careful not to let her lips touch the glass. Could he pull DNA from it? Or from the alcohol swab? She quelled the panic that rose in her chest. She was getting paranoid. He wasn't going to identify her from DNA. She wasn't in the system.

Reilly carefully moved her hair and dabbed at the cut on her head. She flinched at the pain and he murmured an apology. He was being kind and gentle, disarming her defenses. White Knight Syndrome, Carey diagnosed. He liked coming to the aid of a damsel in distress.

"Will you work with a sketch artist?" he asked.

She ignored the stinging as he cleaned her cut. "I didn't see anything."

Detective Truman turned her chair to face him and

crouched down, putting his face close to hers. It was impossible not to notice how gorgeous he was, his dark hair and midnight eyes captivating. Her skin prickled with white-hot awareness.

"I don't believe that. We need to get this guy off the street. You're the first victim to see anything, the second to survive. The other guy's not doing too well. He might not wake up from surgery."

Tension snaked over her shoulders. She wished she could get involved, but she was already too deep into this mess, a mess not of her making. She'd done what she could for the man in the alley and now she had to go back to taking care of herself. If she didn't, no one else would. "I can't," she whispered, her throat tight. His eyes pierced into her, and for a moment she thought he could see to her soul.

If he could, what would he see? A good person? A bad one? A spoiled brat who'd gotten what she'd deserved?

"If you're worried about this guy coming after you, we can provide protection," he said.

Carey wanted to scoff aloud at his naïveté. Maybe they could protect her from a serial killer who worked alone and in the dark of night. But police protection from Mark Sheffield, a man with nearly unlimited resources—nope, not possible. Mark probably had one or two officers in this district already in his pocket. "It's not that."

He inclined his head. "Tell me why. I can help you."

Sadness weighed on her shoulders. Why did it bother her to know she was letting him down? Why did she care what he thought of her? She'd never see him again. "You can't help me. No one can help me."

His face filled with compassion, his eyes soft and

inviting. Did they teach him that in detective school? How to milk the answer he wanted by using his handsome face and beautiful eyes?

"Maybe you don't believe I can help you. But you know in your heart you can help the city. How many innocents are we going to let this guy hurt?"

Carey shifted in her chair, digging her toes into the floor and trying to add some distance between them. She hated how easily she reacted to him and how much she wanted to cooperate when she couldn't. "I want to help you. I do." Her conscience nipped at her heels.

"Then work with a sketch artist."

Carey swallowed. Could she live with herself if she didn't help and the Vagabond Killer struck again? No. She couldn't. "And then I can go home?"

He nodded. "Yes. I'll drive you."

No! "No. I work with the sketch artist and then I leave here alone."

Detective Truman stood upright and rubbed his jaw, considering her offer. "Fine. I'll take what I can get. But my offer stands. If you change your mind, I can give you a ride and I can offer you protection."

Reilly rolled his shoulders, trying to loosen his muscles that were tight and heavy with fatigue. After two hours, Carey Smith, not likely her real name, finished with the sketch artist. She still refused any assistance from him or anyone who had offered. The only thing she had accepted was a candy bar he'd snagged from the vending machine.

Who was she afraid of? An abusive boyfriend? Junkie parents waiting at her apartment? He didn't get addict off her—her arms were clean of track marks, her teeth white and straight, and her skin healthy pink. If not drugs, then what?

She was a contradiction in terms. She claimed to work at Tidy Joe's, where she likely earned less than minimum wage, yet she carried herself with an air of grace that came from careful breeding. Her clothes were cheap and ill-fitting, but she wore them with a flair of style. Her red hair was one of the worst dye jobs he'd seen, but her eyebrows indicated she was naturally blonde. She was beautiful and seemed to make every effort to downplay it.

If Reilly wasn't careful, the next time he saw her, libido would override good sense and he'd reach for her again and wrap his arms around her. And this time, not for medical reasons and not to keep her from running away.

Every sign screamed "woman on the run." Without her real name, he couldn't search through their criminal or missing-persons database. He didn't get any usable prints off the drinking glass or the foil of aspirin she'd taken. The pepper spray was at the lab for analysis. Maybe something would turn up there.

Reilly paced inside his lieutenant's office. He was too tired to sit. If he did, he'd fall asleep and he still needed to escort Carey to her apartment. She could claim independence, she could demand to be left alone, but he wasn't letting her get killed. If he had to, he'd follow at a distance and without her knowing. No one was going to hurt her on his watch.

"How soon do you want the sketch released?" Reilly asked the lieutenant.

The sketch artists were cleaning up the image in preparation for a media blitz. They planned to run the guy's face in every newspaper, every online site and every news broadcast the moment the lieutenant approved it. Even if they couldn't identify the Vagabond Killer from the sketch or from the tip line, the attention might put pressure on the killer and force him to make a mistake. Reilly was certain he wouldn't stop killing until they caught him. And the frequency of his murders was increasing.

The lieutenant scrubbed a hand over his face. "The timing is terrible. Half the staff is taking leave for the holiday. Sending this picture to the media's going to cause a freaking avalanche of insanity. We're having enough trouble manning the tip lines without adding the crazies who think their reclusive neighbor looks somewhat like our guy."

Reilly stopped pacing. "You can count on me to stick around. I'll delay my leave until this guy is caught." His family would understand, and with the new lead and a little luck, maybe they'd close the case by the New Year.

A tap on the door interrupted their discussion. Vanessa Blakely, Assistant D.A., strutted into the office. It was the only way to describe her walk—she strutted, and in heels that looked thin as nails. "I hear we got a witness. Normally, a 3:00 a.m. call puts me in a bad mood, but this I like."

He lifted his eyes from her pointy shoes to her face. "She's with victim assistance, getting some counseling."

Vanessa's eyes clouded with worry. "Is she a street rat?"

Reilly caught the tug of annoyance at her question before he snapped at her. He was tired and hungry and Carey was not a "street rat," Vanessa's term for the homeless at large. "She was walking home from work." Emphasis on the word *work*. He liked Vanessa. She went to bat for victims and she worked hard, but she also had a snobbish streak.

Vanessa let out her breath. "Good, 'cause I can't make a case and use her as a witness if she's a loon."

Her comment lit a faint hint of aggravation in him. "Van, take it down a notch. She interrupted a stabbing in progress, trying to save a stranger and got herself hurt in the process. She could have kept walking. She did a great job with the sketch artist even though she's terrified."

Vanessa set her hand on her hip. "She's a regular superhero. Good to know. Juries love an everyday hero coming to the aid of a victim. Good Samaritan angle."

Vanessa was direct and single-minded about her cases, but she was right about Carey. With the right clothes and a little polishing, Carey would make a witness any jury would adore. If he were on that jury, he'd take one look at her expressive blue eyes, her lush mouth, and with her strength and moxie underscoring her words, he'd swallow the story, hook, line and sinker.

"What's the plan to release the sketch?" Vanessa asked.

The lieutenant set his hands on top of his desk and pushed himself to his feet. He adjusted his belt around his waist. "We were just talking about that. I'm suspending leave for every cop in the city and we'll release the sketch as soon as they have it ready. We'll see if we can pull some volunteers to answer the tip line. The faster it gets out there, the faster we catch this guy."

Reilly snuffed out the last thoughts of taking a six-hour snooze in his bed. It looked like he'd have to settle for a few hours in the bunkhouse and charge up on coffee.

"You gonna tell them or should I?" Reilly asked,

glancing out into the squad room, the gold garland and red stockings they'd tossed up making a mockery of the holiday they weren't going to have until the city was safe.

"I'll do my own dirty work," the lieutenant said. He wiped his brow with his hand, taking the steps into the squad room with more weight than usual. Though the team would grumble about the extra hours, they were dedicated and would do what they were asked to do, holiday or no holiday.

"It's going to be a happy Christmas, huh?" Vanessa asked.

An image of Carey wearing a sexy Santa suit with high black boots, a short skirt and low-cut top flashed into Reilly's mind. He could see her standing beneath twinkling Christmas lights, red and white and hot. He stamped that image out with all his might. He needed to get some rest soon. He couldn't think of victims and witnesses as anything except people involved in his case, which made personal relationships with them off limits. His inconvenient attraction to her would disappear as soon as he'd gotten some sleep.

Ten years ago, his former partner Lucas had made the mistake of becoming emotionally involved with a victim in a case they'd been investigating. When the defense council learned of the relationship, they had twisted it in the eyes of the jury, implying Lucas had coached the victim into giving false testimony. Though Reilly didn't believe the accusation, Lucas had been forced to leave the department, his career in ruins, and a killer had walked free. It had been a brutal lesson for every detective on the squad, one Reilly wouldn't repeat.

Before he could reply to Vanessa, Carey appeared in the squad room, escorted by Officer Dillinger. Strong, yet fragile Carey. She'd relented and worked with the sketch artist, though she'd been under no obligation. She'd been frightened and managed to see the greater good in helping them catch a killer. He respected her a great deal for acting despite her fear.

The air in the room shifted and tensed. Was the unit catching wind their holiday plans were on hold? Or was Carey sending a vibe straight into his gut—a vibe that said protect me, help me, hold me?

Ah, for crying out loud. He needed sleep. Drumming up inappropriate feelings for a witness was a sure sign of extreme exhaustion. The fantasies his mind conjured were delusions. He opened the door to the office and strode across the squad room floor. Vanessa followed close at his back, the clicking of her heels giving her away.

"Hey, Vanessa," Officer Dillinger said, giving Vanessa a long look up and down. "What brings you here?"

Vanessa inclined her head toward Carey. "I came to see if the rumors were true. A living witness."

"Rumors?" Carey asked.

Vanessa waved her hand. "Don't worry. We've kept it out of the media. I have a direct line from the lieutenant's office to my cell."

Officer Dillinger left Carey in their care.

"Will you be able to testify to what you saw after we catch this guy?" Vanessa asked, cutting straight to the point. Vanessa was watching Carey like a cat looking into a goldfish tank, scrutinizing her every move.

Carey's eyes shuttered slightly and warning bells rang in Reilly's head. Whatever came out of her mouth, she was lying. "I'll do what I can."

"Did you give the officers your contact information?" Vanessa asked.

Carey blinked twice, mustering the strength for another lie, Reilly guessed. "Yes."

If she had told them where she lived, it was because she was planning to run.

"And you're sure you don't want police protection? Victim assistance explained the program to you?" Vanessa pressed.

Carey lifted her chin. "I don't need police protection. I saw the Vagabond Killer. He had an eyeful of pepper spray. He didn't see me."

Vanessa appeared impressed. "Great, then you're free to go. I'll be in touch, hopefully soon, to do a lineup." They shook hands and Vanessa strutted through the mass of people, stopping to chat with a few officers working the graveyard shift.

Carey shoved her hands into the pockets of the sweatshirt; her shoulders hunched low as if trying to hide inside her shirt. "I'll see you around."

She appeared small and vulnerable. He had to protect her from whatever had made her afraid. "Let me drive you to your apartment. You can't walk home like that. You'll freeze." The sweatshirt he'd given her wasn't enough to keep her warm in the frigid December cold.

"I'll be fine. I'll take the bus." She glanced away. Lying again. "Besides, I'm used to trekking around in a sweatshirt." Her stomach growled and she pressed a hand over it.

"I can take you somewhere to get something to eat." He couldn't figure her out, her body language shifting from proud to unsure, defiant to willing to help and back again.

"I've got things in my apartment," she said, but she licked her bottom lip as if thinking about food that was most likely not waiting at her place. Reilly weighed pressing her, but not wanting to make her leery, he dropped it. "I'm grateful for what you did today, Carey." Reilly took out his business card. "If you need anything, please give me a call." He'd give her a minute lead and then follow her, make sure she arrived home safely. He didn't have it in him to let her walk away into whatever danger awaited her without trying to help.

She took the card from him and he knew she'd ditch it the second he was out of sight.

"Take care of yourself," he said.

Keeping her gaze to the ground, she walked to the front door. She'd made it halfway across the floor when he rushed after her, a tug in his gut telling him it wasn't a smart idea for her to waltz out the front door of the police station. Vanessa had said she wasn't in the news, but word of another attack might have gotten around the city.

He was five feet behind her and he called her name to stop her. The ringing phones and chatter in the police station drowned out his voice. Carey opened the front door and a flash of cameras and noise exploded in front of her. She whirled in horror and Reilly reached her, tucking her against him, shielding her face from the camera lenses.

The media had snapped a picture of a witness to a serial killing spree.

Chapter 3

"Dillinger, handle that," Reilly barked, pointing to the front door. Dillinger leapt to his feet and went outside to disperse the mob waiting for news of the Vagabond Killer.

Reilly clutched her close to him and she lifted her face. "They took my picture," she said, trembling in his arms.

He tightened his grip on her, wishing he could deny it. But the media was hungry for information and a serial stabbing was front-page news. She could have been a visitor to the precinct for other reasons, but he'd bet at this moment, the media was running her picture through their databases and digging into her life, searching for her identity.

"It's going to be okay," he said. Except rushing to her side made it easy for the media to connect her to the case through him. He swore inwardly.

Carey buried herself tighter against him. "They took my picture," she repeated.

As if in reminder, the sound of reporters clamoring outside seeped into the squad room.

"I can protect you from him," Reilly said, reading the terror in her voice. Holding her felt right, and in the aftermath of their mistake, it was the safest place for her to be. "I shouldn't have let you walk out the door."

Vanessa appeared at his side, wagging her smart phone and looking between the two of them. "Wouldn't have mattered. They were waiting for someone matching her description. The media caught wind there was a witness from someone at the scene. No way can she be alone now. She won't get a moment's rest. They'll stalk her like prey." Vanessa swore under her breath and tapped her foot in agitation.

Carey shoved him away and seemed to shrink lower in her shoes. "I'm fine. If someone could take me home, I'll be fine. No one in the city knows me except my boss and he doesn't watch the news." The tremor in her voice betrayed how scared she was.

Reilly's chest lurched. A woman should never tremble for any other reason than passion. "We can't take chances. You need to go into protective custody."

Carey jammed her hands into her pockets, giving him her shoulder. "I don't think that's necessary."

Reilly turned Carey toward him, nudging her chin up with his finger, meeting her gaze and reading the bottomless well of fear in her eyes. "If you try to do this alone, you won't live through the night."

Vanessa pursed her lips and crossed her arms. "We need you to be someplace where we can find you."

What options did he have? Grungy motel room? His place? One of the overcrowded safe houses? Inspiration dawned on him. "We're unlikely to find an opening in one of our safe houses and the media is going to be everywhere on this one. I'll take you to my parents' place in Montana. It's miles from the nearest town and I can protect you."

Vanessa twisted her lips in thought. "Unconventional, but that's not a bad idea."

Carey shook her head. "I'll be fine. I'll call and let you know where I'll be."

Reilly beat back his frustration. What did it take for her to be *not* fine? She'd witnessed a stabbing, been attacked by a serial killer and harangued by the media. And she claimed she was fine. Leaving Carey alone in the city wasn't an option. The need to protect her intensified.

"Carey, look at me." Carey swiveled her head from Vanessa to him. Reilly met her terror-stricken expression. "I can protect you. I know you don't believe that, maybe because someone's let you down in the past, but I won't. I'm asking you to trust me, which I know is a lot."

She bit her lip and nodded once. "Okay."

That easy? His gut told him she was planning something. "I'll clear it with the lieutenant," Reilly said, not giving either woman time to argue. Most of the hotels in the area were booked with holiday travelers, and getting far away from the media appealed to him immensely. His parents lived in a remote part of Montana on a plot of land difficult to get to, but with a vantage point almost three hundred and sixty degrees around it.

Twenty minutes later, plans in hand, Reilly hustled Carey toward the rear entrance. He stopped in his office to snag his coat and pulled it over her head. She didn't protest and Reilly was relieved she seemed to finally understand the gravity of the situation. This wasn't something she could handle alone. She needed him. "My car's parked in the gated lot in the back. Vanessa had someone clear the area and we're not letting the media behind the building."

"Won't they see me when we pull out?"

"Not if you're covered on the floor."

She quirked up the corners of her mouth. "Are you suggesting I ride in a car without a seat belt?"

Reilly let out a much needed laugh. "Yes, ma'am, that's exactly what I'm suggesting." Her light joke took the edge off his tension.

This was a nightmare, but a serial killer on the loose and the media hounding her was the least of her problems.

Carey gathered her scattered thoughts and took stock of the situation, trying to figure her next move. Walking out of here unescorted with the media waiting wasn't an option and she knew the ADA wouldn't let her leave without a plan of protection. The easiest option was to agree to their plan, and the moment she could, she'd ditch Detective Truman. If she couldn't get rid of him before she left the city, at least it would be more difficult for Mark to track her from some unknown place. She was reasonably sure Detective Truman wasn't on Mark's payroll. Yet.

Detective Truman had pressed her too hard for her name. If he'd been looking for her under Mark's direction, he would have recognized her.

But if Detective Truman threatened her, if she caught even a whiff of betrayal on him, she was gone. She didn't know how or where, but she wouldn't wait around for him to walk her into Mark's trap. Mark had proven he wasn't afraid to use law enforcement, or anyone else, to threaten and intimidate her. This time she would anticipate it. She would be ready.

Her guard was up, and not just for her personal safety. For the safety of those around her she would keep her distance. Mark wouldn't hesitate to hurt someone she cared about in an attempt to get to her. He wouldn't have a problem doling out punishment to those who didn't bend to his will and give him information he wanted.

A pang struck at her chest as memories swept over her. Her good friend Tracy had paid the price for loyalty. Tracy hadn't known where Carey had gone, but she'd known why. When Tracy had shown up in a morgue shortly after Carey went on the run, she'd no question in her mind who was responsible.

Grief and anger burned red hot in Carey's gut. She'd had to run. The life she'd known had been stripped from her, people she'd loved had died, and Mark was living on easy street, running the restaurants and wineries her father had owned.

Carey wouldn't let Mark find her. If he did, she was dead.

The moment Carey opened the door to her apartment, Reilly's senses went on heightened alert. Flour dusted the floor near the entrance, likely a cheap mechanism to know if someone had been inside. An unknowing intruder would step directly into it and leave a print. That flour wasn't for the Vagabond Killer. He'd been right—Carey was running from someone. An abusive ex?

Carey went into the apartment first, taking a wide step over the flour. "Watch your step."

No further explanation about the flour? He avoided the powdery mess and followed her inside.

Her apartment was a tiny closet of a space with no

personal items and nothing unpacked or settled. A ten-inch television sat on a packing crate and a cot in the corner of the room served as her bed. The floor was matted with grime, the vinyl likely original from when this building was constructed in the '70s. The place smelled of citrus, as though she'd used a gallon of lemon-scented cleaner in a futile attempt to make the place livable.

She shrugged off his coat and handed it to him. "I need a few minutes to pack and I'd like some privacy. Do you mind waiting in the car?"

Private person, or was she hiding something?

"Not a problem. I'll wait in the lobby. I can see the stairs from there."

She gave him a thin smile and practically pushed him out the door. He returned to his car and circled the block, pulling into the alley behind the building. No way was she planning to meet him in the lobby of the building. She planned to run, and he would be hot on her trail.

Sure as the sun, ten minutes later, he saw her fling her slim jeans-clad leg over the window ledge and her body drop onto the fire escape. With a large duffel bag slung across her shoulder, she climbed down the rusty ladder to each landing. Her fierce persistence to get away gave him insight into the passion and resolve simmering beneath those plain clothes. What was she hiding or who was she protecting?

He got out of his car and jogged to meet her at the foot of the fire escape. "Going on a trip?"

She whirled, fear in her eyes. She wiped her hands on her jeans, leaving behind bits of paint and rust that had stuck to her palms. "I need to go for a walk to clear my head."

He called her bluff. "Great, I'll walk with you."

"I prefer to be alone," she said through clenched teeth. She walked around him and started down the alley toward the main road.

He followed her. "It doesn't matter what you prefer. The lieutenant assigned me to protect you and that's what I'm going to do."

She paused for a moment, stopping in her tracks. She looked over her shoulder at him, her blue eyes narrowed. "Don't make this harder on me than it has to be. I gave you what you needed. You have your sketch of the Vagabond Killer. Do your job and find him."

He chose his words carefully, not wanting to provoke her further. "We need your testimony."

She hefted the bag higher on her shoulder, wincing slightly. "The ADA's smart. She'll figure something out." She kept walking, stopping at the corner to wait for the light to change. "Stop following me, Detective. I'm not a suspect and I'm not required to stay in the city."

He'd known she'd agreed to his protection too easily. "Tell me where you're going."

"It's safer for both of us if no one knows."

Reilly grabbed her elbow, stopping her in her tracks. "Let me help you."

He held her gaze for a long, intense moment. Heat pulsed between them and arousal moved swiftly through his body. What was it about her, a simple touch, one smoldering look that made him ache for more? He wished the fabric of the sweatshirt wasn't between them and he could feel the electric press of skin-to-skin contact.

He didn't let go and she didn't pull away. "He'll kill you if you try to hide me. Don't make me live with that on my conscience."

The Vagabond Killer would have to find her first. And Reilly was good at hiding in plain sight. He was even better at it when he had options, places to disappear in the country. And if she was referring to whoever made her put flour by the door coming for him, it was laughable. He welcomed the attack of a woman abuser. It would give him the opportunity to pound some scum and give him what he deserved. "No one is going to kill me, and if I'm with you, no one is going to hurt you, either." He let go of her arm.

She looked around, her expressive eyes wild. "Look, I'll level with you because I'm in a hurry. Those reporters who took my picture are going to run it in the news, if they haven't already. That means the man I'm running from will see it and come for me. I have to get out of town before he arrives."

Not the Vagabond Killer. She was worried about her abuser. "Tell me his name."

She shook her head. "I can't do that."

Loyalty to the man who hurt her? Nah, she didn't seem like the type. Fear. She actually thought the man chasing her was that powerful. "I'm taking you out of town to someplace safe."

"Thank you, but no." The light changed and she crossed the street.

Reilly heard the fierce determination in her voice. She wasn't going to give in and he couldn't legally force her to comply. He tried another route to convince her. "Once he knows you're in Denver, he'll know you took public transportation out of here. How long before he narrows down where you went? Someone is bound to remember you."

She huffed out a breath. "Stop trying to scare me. I'll change buses and trains fifty times if I have to."

"That's expensive and you can't make that much working at a Laundromat. My family's ranch is safe. My father's a retired Navy SEAL, my mom is ex-CIA, one of my brothers is military and the other is FBI. The ranch is remote, it's protected and we'll see someone coming for you. You'll be safe with us."

He glanced at her face and instantly regretted pressing her.

Carey's cheeks were red and her eyes brimmed with tears. "What if he comes and he hurts you for helping me?"

His protective instinct plowed through him and he kept his hands pinned to his sides, a massive undertaking considering he wanted to hold her and offer some measure of comfort. "He won't. He'll be dead if he comes within fifty feet of the house."

She brushed at her eyes with the sleeve of his sweatshirt. His sweatshirt. He'd gotten it years before, after he'd graduated from the academy. Funny, he had never allowed anyone—not his ex-girlfriends, not his former fiancée—to wear it. Yet seeing Carey shivering in his office, he hadn't thought twice about offering it to her.

"I won't tell you anything about my past."

He shrugged. He got the gist of the picture. Scum chasing his victim. His beautiful, and at the moment, fragile victim. He guessed under other circumstances, she was a force to be reckoned with. "I won't ask."

"How do you know I'm not running from the law?" she asked.

Her lips parted slightly and he was momentarily distracted by the lush fullness of them. He forced his attention to her eyes. He found them as mesmerizing as her lips. "Gut feeling. Trumans live by it. You're no more a criminal than I am."

* * *

"Come on inside with me," Detective Truman said. He'd pulled his car into his garage and closed the door using the remote on his car visor. "I need to grab a few things. Clothes. Ammunition. I'll make it fast before the media swarm starts."

The media might be tracking her, but Detective Truman would have caught their interest, as well. That a camp of reporters weren't waiting on his porch was a small favor.

He was taking precautions to make her feel safer, but traveling a long distance with a stranger and a gun made her nervous.

She had to be crazy to agree to his plan. Sure, he'd been kind to her thus far, but what did she really know about him? He was a police detective; that in and of itself didn't mean he was trustworthy. If he wasn't on Mark's payroll, he could be added. Finding and exploiting a person's weakness was a specialty of Mark's. It was only a matter of time before Mark got to Detective Truman. Either Mark would buy him off or, if Detective Truman resisted, Mark would kill him. Carey couldn't live with herself knowing she'd caused another person to be hurt. Tracy's face flashed into her mind and Carey braced herself against the wave of grief and guilt that crashed down on her.

Detective Truman was doing this because he needed her to testify against the Vagabond Killer. But that wasn't going to happen. If they both lived to see the Vagabond Killer brought to trial, testifying meant telling the truth about who she was—and that wasn't possible.

"I can wait here if you want. I don't want to intrude." Was this her last chance to run? Could she get out of the car and force open the door to the garage? How far would she get on foot?

"Nah, you're fine. I'll feel better having you in sight."

Carey had nowhere else to go and no one else to turn to for help. If she ran, her limited resources meant Mark would find her. She didn't want to get Detective Truman involved in her personal problems, but witnessing a crime had meshed their lives together, if only for a short time.

And while Carey didn't trust easily or often, her instincts told her she would be safe with Detective Truman for now. Not that she relied too heavily on her instincts. She'd been wrong about Mark, wrong about her father and wrong about so many things before.

She'd keep her time with Detective Truman short—a few days at most. He'd get her out of the city and make it easier to run without Mark following her.

She trailed him inside the house. It was a bachelor pad, but a clean one. No knickknacks and no pictures. He didn't have a kitchen table, likely eating his meals at the breakfast bar or in the living room on his black leather couch. She wrinkled her nose. Black leather. Blah.

"What's the matter?" he asked, catching her expression.

"Nothing."

"It's okay, you can tell me. Do you need something? Is your arm bothering you?"

Her arm was fine. Her ribs were throbbing, but she wasn't fixating on that. "It's your couch." She blushed, regretting her criticism. It wasn't like her apartment would be featured in a home decorating magazine anytime soon.

He glanced into the living room, a look of confusion on his face. "What about it?"

Polite response? "It's so manlike."

Detective Truman tossed her a crooked grin. "I am a man."

Yes, he was. A big one. A handsome one. Impossible not to notice.

He grinned at her. "Try it," he said, gesturing toward the couch.

Had she spoken aloud? "What?"

"Have a seat. Flip on the TV. You'll see the magic. I'm going to grab a few things from upstairs. I'll be down in a minute."

"Okay." Carey wandered into the living room and plopped down on the couch. It wasn't what she'd expected. She'd thought leather couches were for frat boys and playboys, but this was nice. She ran her hands over the cushion and inhaled the smell of it. It was supple and soft. Her nerves shot lust into her veins. Yeah, the couch was magic.

How many women had fallen under Detective Truman's charms in this exact place? And why did it bother her to think about him spending the night curled up with a woman?

Carey picked up the remote from the coffee table and flipped on the television. Sports network. Of course. She leaned back, letting her body sink into the plush cushions. She nearly let out a moan, somewhere between pleasure and pain. The pain in her ribs intensified when she reclined and since the aspirin had worn off and without adrenaline propelling her, her body caved in to the ache.

"Comfortable?" Detective Truman asked.

Carey opened her eyes and straightened. "It's nice."

Detective Truman dropped his bag on the floor and sat next to her. "Perfect place to watch football."

"My father used to…" She let her voice drift away. It had been a long time since she'd spoken of her father and the mention of him cut to the quick. The rawness hadn't gone away and the wound seeped inside her chest. She forced down her grief, trying to think about something else as she fought tears.

"It's okay to let it out," Detective Truman said, tucking his arm around her shoulder. "You've been through a rough time."

He had no idea. The heaviness in her chest was suffocating. "My father died recently."

"I'm sorry," he said into her hair, moving her closer to him.

His hand rubbed her shoulder, providing comfort she hadn't had in months. She sank against him, needing this more than she'd realized.

"I miss him sometimes." All the time. A constant yearning she'd only dealt with by ignoring it when she could.

"Is that why you're alone?" he asked, his voice unbearably tender, his fingers massaging her with the right amount of pressure and gentleness, her body relaxing under his touch.

Tears she'd fought spilled over and she pressed her face into his shoulder, hiding them. After all these months, she should have healed more, should have been coping better. The heart-wrenching grief hadn't loosened its hold. "Yes. It's why I'm alone." Without her father, her world had fallen apart. Her good friend had died in a car accident. The people she had trusted left her. Mark had betrayed her. Her life as she knew it had ended.

Detective Truman stroked her hair gently and reached for a tissue on the side table. He palmed her chin and dabbed at her eyes. "You're not alone anymore."

Everything in her responded to his words. Her heart surged and her mind cried out with pleasure. As desperate as it was, they were words she had longed to hear. She didn't need forever; she needed not to feel this lonely for a little while. So many reasons to keep her distance from this man and yet she reached for him, skimming her fingers down his arm to his hand. He tensed slightly but didn't pull away. He was too handsome for his own good, said all the right things, and his confidence drew her, awakening her slumbering desire, tempting her to touch him, taste him.

She moved her hand under his. "Detective Truman?"

He looked at their joined hands. "Reilly. Just Reilly." His voice was gruff. She affected him. It sent a secret thrill across her belly.

"Reilly." His name rolled across her tongue. "Why are you doing this?"

He swallowed hard. "Doing what?"

She leaned closer to him. "You don't have to take care of me." But she loved that he was.

"I know."

"Then why are you?"

"Gut feeling."

She moved her fingers to interlace with his, in part to test his reaction. His jaw flexed and he looked at her. His eyes were filled with emotions she couldn't read.

A second later Reilly came to his feet, pulling his hand away, and she fell forward on the couch, catching herself on her hands. Her arm burned, slamming her back into reality.

He looked blankly away from her at some point on the wall. "We need to get moving."

What had she been trying to do? Touching him that way had been a mistake. She was lonely and hurting and she'd made an error in judgment. His rejection stung worse than it should have. She stood, humiliation darkening her cheeks. "I'm sorry, I shouldn't have touched you."

Reilly waved his hand dismissively. "Don't mention it again. You're going through a rough time."

Carey swallowed hard and blotted out the sense of longing he'd roused. She'd been going through a rough time for too long. She couldn't explain it, not without sounding like an overemotional lunatic, so she stayed quiet and followed him to his car. Working to put herself together, she focused on getting out of the city and where she'd go and what she'd do next.

Staying with Reilly wasn't possible, not without one or both of them getting hurt.

Chapter 4

Carey fiddled with the car's radio buttons, looking for a station with music that wouldn't worsen her headache or make the mood in the car too mushy. She was already feeling exposed, having made the mistake of holding Reilly's hand and being rejected. Setting the wrong tone made her feel embarrassed all over again. He wasn't behaving as if it was a big deal and she tried to write it off in her mind. Mistake with a capital M.

He was a good-looking man and he wasn't interested in her. She could handle that. She could move on. She was an expert at moving on.

Her hand froze over the dial when she heard the Vagabond Killer mentioned.

"...known as the Vagabond Killer. The Denver police are questioning a witness who survived one of the killer's attacks and is reportedly able to identify him."

Embarrassment rushed out of her and was replaced by fear.

Reilly reached for her hand and moved it away from the radio dial. "Let's switch to satellite radio. We don't need to hear the news."

The contact sent plumes of fire licking at her skin. She set her hands in her lap. A casual touch shouldn't evoke a heated response. "They were talking about the case. It's already hit the streets. I'll bet my picture is everywhere."

"We knew this would happen and that's why we're leaving the city. There's nothing you can do about the case now, so try to put it out of your mind."

Carey closed her eyes and took a deep breath. The case she could block. The possibility that Mark was en route to Denver to find her chilled her to the core. Could Reilly protect her? She glanced at him, taking in the rough cut angles of his face and the strength of his body. Good looking didn't begin to describe him. Carey had trouble pretending her attraction to him was nil. What mattered most was his ability to protect her, his strength, and the street smarts to keep one step ahead of someone tracking her. He seemed to have a surplus of that. The handsome part she needed to forget.

They drove for an hour, the radio playing an endless stream of songs. Carey focused on the lyrics, anything not to think about Mark hunting her. Reilly finally broke the silence between them. "I need to stop and get some coffee." He turned the car onto the off ramp of the interstate.

"I could drive for a while if you want," Carey said. He looked tired and she wondered when he'd last slept.

He raised his eyebrow. "Do you have a driver's license?"

"No." She'd had a driver's license and a nice car, but those things were a part of the past. Carey Smith had neither.

"Then, no, you can't drive." His voice was tinted with amusement.

They drove into a gas station and he pulled into one of the parking spaces next to the minimart. Only one other car was parked, another filling up their tank at the gas pump.

Reilly turned off the ignition. "You want anything to eat?"

"Sure. I could go for some food."

He'd grabbed a box of crackers from his house before they'd left and she'd eaten most of them. She mentally calculated how much money she had and figured she could spare a dollar or two from the emergency cash jammed in her duffel bag.

They went inside, Reilly threading through the aisles of snack foods and traveler conveniences to the coffee bar. Carey kept her head down as she followed after him. The store was mostly empty, but she didn't want to chance anyone recognizing her.

The coffee smelled as if it had been sitting since the morning, brown stains burnt to the side of the glass pots. Reilly didn't seem to mind and he snatched a gallon-sized jug from the line of cups and filled it, adding sugar and cream. He gestured around the store. "Get anything you want. We have another seven hours on the road."

Carey's stomach growled and she took Reilly's advice, picking up a bag of pretzels and a bag of gummy worms. Reilly added a few items to their order, including some shrink-wrapped subs with wilted lettuce. He insisted on paying. They gathered their stash and returned to the car.

"Thank you for this," she said, gesturing to the food in her lap.

"It's nothing."

But it was something to her. No one had bought her anything in the last year. Not a birthday present. Not a greeting card. Her throat grew tight. His kindness touched her deeply. He'd think she was overreacting, so she turned her attention to the window.

He pulled to the filling station and got out to pump his gas. Carey tore into her gummy worms.

She watched Reilly, his torso visible through the window. He was a magnificent specimen of a man, and beneath his jacket and dress shirt, she guessed she'd find pumped biceps and a tight stomach. What woman wouldn't take notice? Not that she had delusions about him. He'd made it clear he wasn't interested in pursuing a physical relationship with her and she doubted he desired any relationship at all. She didn't blame him.

She was lonely. Needy. On the run. Her life was a mess. He had his together.

But he had ignited something in her blood. He made her feel alive. And she liked how it felt to be back among the living. She imagined kissing him, running her hands over his bare skin, nibbling on his earlobes. Nothing so detailed that she got lost in her fantasies, but enough to keep tension humming in her veins.

If Reilly kissed her, his lips would be soft, yet firm, commanding and giving, hungry and satisfying. His mouth would close over hers and in that moment, he would own her. And if they made love, she would climb on top of him and then she would own him. She smiled at the idea, at owning a man like Reilly, even for a night. Undoubtedly, it would be amazing.

But Reilly had other ideas. They were witness and detective, plain and simple, and Reilly seemed intent on keeping it that way.

Carey fell asleep curled against the inside of the car door, another sweatshirt she'd pulled from her duffel across her upper body like a blanket, her empty bags of food on the floor by her feet.

No one had followed them from Denver. For long stretches of highway, they'd been alone.

Reilly took another swallow of coffee and glanced over at her serene face, the red hair falling across it. For the hundredth time that day, he wondered about her, about the man she was terrified of and why she thought running was the only option. In the short time he'd known her she seemed to behave like two different women. Scared Carey, who wanted to flee and hide, was a direct contrast to bold Carey, who had interrupted a stabbing in progress, who'd stroked his arm with delicate fingers, who'd smirked at him in a way that made his mind leap to all kinds of lusty possibilities. His gaze did a slow slide down her body.

She had a "come here and touch me" look. A look he had to ignore. Of course his body had its own ideas about what he should do and most of its suggestions had everything to do with touching her.

Reilly had to maintain his objectivity and getting involved with a woman—especially a witness—would cloud his judgment and compromise the investigation. He couldn't allow the Vagabond Killer to remain on the streets on a technicality. Like one of the detectives on the case sleeping with a witness.

Carey would be safe with him and his family until they caught the guy and brought Carey in to do a lineup.

Only Vanessa and the lieutenant knew he was planning to take her to his parents' ranch outside Ashland, and Carey had told him she didn't need to contact anyone before leaving. That hadn't surprised him. People on the run didn't make friends and they didn't trust easily.

But she had trusted him when she'd agreed to come to his family's home. He wouldn't take that trust lightly and would do everything he could to keep it.

He hadn't given his family a head's up, but he knew they'd be okay with it. It was easier to explain in person. His family would help him protect Carey and give her a safe place to hide until the Vagabond Killer was caught. They'd also be discreet in keeping her presence a secret. She didn't just need protection from the Vagabond Killer; she needed to be kept safe from the man looking for her.

Reilly nudged away the urge to press her for details about her past. He'd promised he wouldn't, but the investigator in him hated unanswered questions. Who was this man and what about him scared her so much?

Carey was beautiful. Strong. Courageous. Her baggy clothes were an obvious attempt to draw attention away from her curvy body. He knew what was beneath those clothes. When the EMT had been examining her, Reilly had seen the flatness of her belly, felt the softness of her skin and noticed the roundness of her breasts.

He shifted in his seat, turned down the heat in the car and adjusted his pants, which suddenly felt too tight. He'd promised to protect her, not ravage her. It didn't matter how beautiful she was or how much he ached to kiss her.

She was a perpetual temptation he had to ignore. The case had to come first. Getting a killer off the streets would save lives. Reilly took his duty as an officer of the law seriously and with that came a code of conduct he wouldn't violate, no matter how beautiful the temptation.

He took another sip of coffee, which had long turned cold. It wasn't that good to start with, but he'd needed something to keep him awake. He swallowed the bitter brew and concentrated on the road ahead of him.

After driving another two hours and drinking too much coffee, Reilly needed to use the bathroom and stretch his legs. Signs on the highway had announced a rest area nearby. Seeing the entrance, he pulled off the road and for a moment, he considered leaving Carey sleeping in the car. The rest stop had a few cars clustered around the main building and several large tractor trailers parked in the rear of the lot. After the trauma she'd suffered, waking her when she looked peaceful and comfortable seemed unfair. He hated to do it. But it was better if she came with him.

Even in a sweatshirt and jeans, her hair tied back with pieces loose in the front, she was one of the most enthralling women he'd seen. He spoke her name several times and then touched her arm lightly. "Carey."

She opened her eyes and shifted, looking around, confusion lighting her face. "Are we there?"

He shook his head. They had hours to go before they reached Ashland. "No, I need to use the restroom." The strain of exhaustion showed around her eyes and Reilly regretted waking her.

She straightened and pulled her hood over her head, covering her red hair. "Good idea."

They climbed out of the car and walked in the main door of the rest stop. Reilly stayed close, wanting her within arm's reach. A healthy dose of paranoia could save her life, and the idea of her walking alone in the open, unprotected, didn't sit well with him.

The building was stark with whitewashed block walls and a cement floor, but it had the basics—a display of maps and points-of-interest brochures, a few vending and soda machines, and men's and women's bathrooms.

"When you're done, wait for me here," he said, pointing to the vending machines. "Don't go outside. I'll be around the corner in the men's room." He hated for her to be alone, but he couldn't go into the bathroom with her.

Carey nodded. "I'll be careful. I promise."

Reilly watched her enter the women's room and then hurried to the men's room. The fewer seconds she was out of his sight, the better.

Carey glanced over her shoulder as she entered the women's room. Reilly was waiting for her to go inside. The area wasn't crowded and she didn't see anyone she recognized—a good sign. Mark was looking for her, and while she'd known that since she'd run months ago, her picture on the news would give him plenty of clues about her whereabouts.

How far had she and Reilly traveled from Denver? It had to be a least a hundred miles. Was the distance enough that Mark and his thugs would lose her trail?

Carey hurried to finish in the bathroom and washed her hands at the sink. She splashed some water on her face and patted it dry with a paper towel. The mirror was smeared and dirty, speckled with chips and brown age spots, but from what she could see, she looked like something a cat threw up. She turned away. There was nothing she could do about her appearance now.

Another woman entered and as the door swung open,

Carey glanced out. Two men she recognized were waiting by the door, their arms crossed, serious expressions on their faces. The shorter man had a goatee and the taller, broader man was clean shaven. She struggled to place them in her memory and to recall their names. Bits and pieces fell into place. When she'd met them for the first time, what had struck her most were their cold, dead eyes. Mark's associates. They weren't friends of Mark. They were his hired muscle.

How had they found her? Terror clutched at her chest. She had to warn Reilly. But how? She didn't have a phone to call him and if she borrowed a phone, she didn't know his number. If she walked out of the bathroom, even with her head down and her hood pulled up, they would see her. What if they saw Reilly coming out of the bathroom? Would they attempt to hurt him? Did they know to look for him?

She scanned the room for a weapon to defend herself. Toilet paper, paper towels and a few deodorizers were useless. But there was a window. It was small and higher on the wall, but if she flipped over the trash can and used it as a stool, she could pop the window and climb out.

The other woman in the bathroom shot her a strange look as she dragged the trash can toward the window. Carey didn't care. She needed to hurry and get to Reilly before they did.

Standing on the trash can, she unlocked the window. It was an old window, pivoting from the bottom and swinging out at the top. She gave it a firm push, but it didn't budge. She shoved it again, wondering when it had last been opened. If the dust, cobwebs and grime were any indication, it had been months. Maybe years. The window groaned and she worked her fist around its edges like a hammer, loosening it. With a final swing, the window opened and cool air rushed in.

It was a tight fit, but Carey was determined to squeeze through. Putting weight on her ribs burned, but she quelled the cry of pain that sprang to her lips. If Mark's thugs heard a commotion in the bathroom, they might come to investigate and see her half-dangling out the window.

Contorting her already bruised body, she managed to slide through the open window and fall to the ground outside the bathroom. She landed on her side, her hip striking first. Ignoring the stinging pain, she dragged herself to her feet and circled the building, looking for another entrance.

Behind the rest area was a small patio with wooden picnic benches…and a door leading inside. One small element in her favor. She rushed to it, pulling on the handle. It gave and she opened it a few inches, peering through the crack.

Mark's men's heads were bent together in quiet discussion. Wondering if they should charge inside the women's restroom and look for her?

Her heart sank when she saw Reilly standing by the vending machines. If the thugs turned around, they'd see him. Reilly glanced at his watch. Was he getting worried about why she was taking so long? How could she signal him without calling attention to herself?

Carey closed her eyes and prayed for a distraction. Where was the large bus trip making a stop and flooding the area? In the confusion, she could get to Reilly and they could hightail it to Montana.

No large flood of people came, nor any other distraction, but losing their patience, the thugs made a move to enter the women's bathroom. Carey's legs seemed to think for themselves. She shoved open the door and raced toward Reilly. He turned to her, either hearing the footsteps or sensing her approach. Pressing a finger over her lips, she pointed to the front doors. He cocked his head in question, but didn't speak.

They had three seconds before the thugs figured out she wasn't in the bathroom and started looking for her. Taking Reilly's hand and ignoring the surge of heat in his touch, she ran with him toward the door.

When they were outside, he stopped, setting his hands on her arms, forcing her to face him. "What's going on? What are you—"

She cut him off and ignored the heat lightning that ricocheted between them at the contact. They didn't have time for delay. "Someone from my past has found me."

His eyes narrowed in thought. "Are you sure?"

Yes, she was sure. She didn't know how they had found her, but they had. "Please, we have to go. They can't know where we're headed, or nowhere is safe." She took his sleeve and tugged him in the direction of his car. He followed her.

Reilly swore under his breath. "I didn't see anyone tailing us."

It didn't matter now. All that mattered was getting away. "We'll worry about the how later. Please, let's just go!"

Reilly drew her to a stop. "Which car is theirs?"

Carey scanned the parking lot. A minivan. A Cadillac. And the black sports car. "The black car." The one parked a space down from Reilly's white sedan.

Reilly dragged his keys from his pocket and opened the pocketknife attached to his key ring. He pressed the button to unlock his car doors. "Get inside the car."

He went to the front tire of the black car and slit the rubber. Then he did the same to the back tire. Hearing a shout, Carey looked to the entrance of the building. The thugs had seen them and were racing in their direction.

"Hurry," Carey yelled from the passenger seat.

Reilly circled his car and got inside, started the engine and zipped out of the spot. Carey couldn't tear her eyes from the side mirror. The thugs climbed in their car, prepared to give chase.

"Why did you slit both tires?" she asked. The seconds might have cost them.

"In case they have a spare. They won't have two," he said, his jaw tight with tension.

Turning in her seat to watch behind them, fear drained from her chest when they skidded to the side of the road. "They stopped."

Reilly swore under his breath and banged his fist against the steering wheel. "I made a rookie mistake. They must have followed my electronic trail."

"What mistake?" she asked. Was it a mistake that would cost their lives? "Did they follow your cell? Your pager?"

"No, my cell is department-issued. The signal bounces across cell towers at random locations across the country. But I used my credit card at the minimart on 59. We're still traveling on 59. If someone was watching my cards, they would have gotten the location." He glanced at her, his face filled with questions. "Someone who can trace credit card activity must be serious about finding you."

Panic swelled inside her. How could she answer that without giving away too much information?

She got lucky and Reilly didn't wait for her to answer. She was faintly aware of him calling the police.

But most of her was reeling in relief at having escaped another close call with Mark.

Taking back roads to his family's house added a few hours to the drive, but Reilly wasn't taking chances more men had been stationed along the main highway looking for his car. The near miss at the rest stop had convinced him that the man—or men—after Carey meant business.

The ranch came into view in the distance, atop a hill accessible by vehicle via one road that scaled to the summit, weaving across the terrain. His father would see him as he drove closer to home, no trees blocking the view. The final few miles of the trip brought the familiarity and comforts of home.

Carey stirred when he stopped the car in front of the house and burrowed deeper beneath her blanket sweatshirt. He touched her arm and she started, turning in her seat, her eyes wide.

He was quick to reassure her. "You're okay. We're at my family's house."

She pressed her hand over her heart. "Sorry, I'm a little jumpy."

What must it be like for her to live in a constant state of fear? To never have a sense of family and security? She must live one day to the next, no plans for the future, spending her time running from the past. After being chased from the rest stop, her fears of being found didn't seem as extreme as he'd first believed. The man searching for her was dangerously dedicated to finding her. Reilly wanted to find the words to reassure her that everything would work out. He'd see to it. "You'll be safe here. My family has over three hundred acres of land and the nearest town is over ten miles away. We live in the middle of nowhere."

An uneasy expression crossed her face and it dawned on him she might fear being alone with a man without a place to flee. So much for finding the right words. "My mom will love having another woman in the house," he added.

She sat up, unbuckling her seat belt. "I'm sorry I wasn't good company on the drive. I was so tired."

Reilly made a sound of acknowledgment and didn't bother mentioning he was dead on his feet. He looked toward the house, up to the second-floor front window of his bedroom. The brick chimney smoked into the cold air and Reilly smiled at the thought of a warm bed, a hot cup of cocoa and a huge homemade meal. His mom was great at keeping food around for him, his dad and his brothers. The refrigerator and pantry would be stocked in preparation for the holidays.

They got out of the car and Reilly carried her duffel and his bag to the front porch. He rang the bell once and his mother pulled the door open, her arms extended.

Letting out an exclamation of joy, she hugged Reilly close. "And you brought a friend with you." The word *friend* hung thick with implication. Reilly ignored it. He'd explain later the reasons she was here. For now he wanted Carey to feel at home.

"Mom, this is Carey. Carey, this is my mom, Jane."

Jane took Carey's hands in hers. "It's a pleasure to meet you. Come inside and we'll get you settled." Jane moved away from the door to allow them entrance.

"Thank you for having me," Carey said, stepping across the threshold and wiping her feet on the mat.

"I welcome anyone who's a friend of my son," Jane

said. Again the word *friend* came with a questioning look to Reilly.

Twenty minutes later his mother had taken Carey upstairs and decided she would sleep in his old bedroom. "You and Harris can bunk in his room," Jane said with a smile.

His mom was pleased he'd brought a friend to visit, but Jane was as old-fashioned as June Cleaver. No sleepovers with girls, even if her sons were well into their thirties.

Reilly shrugged at his mom, letting her know the arrangement was fine even if the image of Carey stretched out in his bed beside him brought fresh waves of heat washing over him. A ridiculous thought. He and Carey weren't a couple; he was handling this situation with complete professionalism, and going to bed with her was out of the question. Harris's room was close enough that he could keep an eye on her and be at her side in seconds if anything happened.

"Get yourselves settled. Dinner is in a few hours." Jane walked from the room, leaving the door to the bedroom ajar.

"I guess your mom was surprised to see me," Carey said.

Dang, she was pretty. Those brilliant blue eyes could speak right to a man's soul. Why couldn't she have been utterly unappealing? "I don't bring women around often."

"You could have explained why I'm here."

Reilly rolled his shoulders. "I will. Soon. Right now I need a nap." Alone. To get his thoughts together and focus on the case.

Worry filled her eyes. "When's the last time you had some sleep?"

He glanced at his watch. "Too long ago. I didn't want to waste time napping when we needed to get out of the city."

Carey looked at the floor and the impulse to draw her into his arms rocked him. Lack of sleep was making his thoughts hazy, centering around the idea of her spooned against him, his arms around her. Warmth. Comfort. Happiness.

Simple things he missed having with a woman. Taking naps together on cool sheets on lazy afternoons. Gentle wake-up kisses in the morning. Sleeping in late and having breakfast at noon. Things he hadn't shared with a woman in years. Hadn't missed in years.

Years? Had it really been that long since he'd been in a relationship? He'd had casual flings, quick rolls in the sack to sate his physical urges. He'd had sex with zero emotional connection, but hadn't shared anything real with a woman in too long.

Yeah, he definitely needed sleep. He was getting overemotional and weepy, thinking about chick stuff. Next thing he knew, he'd be buffing his nails and blow-drying his hair.

"Would it be okay if I took a shower?" Carey asked. "I've got two days of grime on me."

"Do you need help?" he asked, remembering the injuries on her head and arm. Seeing her alarmed expression, he hurriedly added, "With your bandages. My mom could give you a hand." Though his body responded to the image of her naked, and his hands running soap over her, he quashed it. Wasn't going to happen. What she needed now was some sense of safety and the freedom to relax. He didn't want her to feel afraid at the Truman Ranch. He didn't know how, but he was going to take care of her and give her back her life.

Carey shook her head. "No, I can manage. I'm fine."

There was that word again. *Fine*. Was she really fine? Or was she hungry? In pain? "I'll get you a towel. Do you need anything else?"

He knew she'd decline and she did. "No, but thank you for bringing me here. I don't know where else I could have gone."

He reached out and cupped her cheek, the lightest of touches, careful to be exceedingly gentle. She inhaled sharply and stiffened, but after a few moments, she relaxed. He'd intended the gesture to set her at ease, to assure her she could trust him. It had the unintended effect of sending desire blazing through him. Every time they touched, the sultry hum of anticipation buzzed in his ears. Telling himself nothing could happen, not now, not ever, didn't silence it.

"I'll protect you, Carey. You don't have to be scared."

Their gazes connected in a hot, devouring stare. Her eyes never leaving his, she turned her head and kissed the inside of his wrist.

His body flared with heat, excitement pooling in his lower extremities. A kiss of gratitude? Did she think she owed him something for helping her? He'd met women who'd never been given kindness without an expectation of a return favor. Is that what this was?

He dropped his hand and stepped away. No matter how appealing she was, no matter how badly he wanted her beneath him, he had to keep some boundaries between them, maintain a professional distance to let her know she was safe here and no one expected she pay them back.

"I'll get you a towel," he said quickly and put space between them before he threw his code of honor out the window, caved to his raging hormones and kissed her.

* * *

Carey peeled off her shoes and socks, grateful for the opportunity to bathe in a spotless shower. The one in her apartment had never made her feel clean. The water pressure hadn't been good, the hot water lasted only a few minutes, and the stains on the walls and tub couldn't be bleached away. She knew. She had tried endlessly to scrub them.

The bathroom adjoined Reilly's bedroom, where she would be sleeping, and his brother's room, where he would be staying. One door separated the bathroom from where she presumed Reilly was napping. She was careful about every noise she made, trying not to make a racket and keep him awake. Then again, he had needed rest and might have stumbled into bed and fallen dead asleep.

A refreshing shower would help her clear her head and settle her nerves. The terror of seeing Mark's goons, the adrenaline rush of escaping, the surge of desire when she was close to Reilly mixed in her mind, confusing and exhausting her.

Lifting her arms over her head to remove her shirt made the side of her ribs ache and she squelched a cry of pain that rose to her lips. She hadn't had time to examine her injuries fully since the incident in the alley. Easing the shirt over her head, she folded it and set it on the floor. She inspected her back and her side in the bathroom mirror, both dark purple with bruises. She pulled her hair free of the elastic holding it and angled a hand mirror to examine her scalp in the bathroom mirror. Thanks to Reilly, the back of her head wasn't a clotted bloody mess, but it needed to be tended to again.

She looked at herself directly in the mirror and nearly gasped. Her dyed red hair hung limp around her head and dark rings circled her eyes. She looked gaunt and tired, the scrape on her chin red and raw. She hadn't had a haircut in a salon in a year. Only the grown-out layers lingering in her hair gave it any shape. Trips to the salon for a trendy haircut belonged in her old life; she didn't have time or money to be vain. She carefully removed the bandage from her arm and examined the cut. The butterfly stitches had held.

The care Reilly had shown her, cleaning her cut, asking about her injuries, amounted to another point in his favor, another reason she liked him. Reilly Truman was the whole package: great career, great family, great protector and gorgeous, to boot. The chemistry between them wouldn't quit. One touch of his hand had nearly unhinged her.

Powerful, undeniable chemistry with a cop. Just what she needed to make this situation more difficult to navigate.

She was lucky to be alive and grateful to be here with Reilly and his butt-kicking family. She wouldn't have agreed to come, worried she would lure danger to them, but he'd presented his family like a team of superheroes. They could take care of themselves, and she wouldn't be around for long. Maybe a few days at most, enough time for the worst of her wounds to heal. Then she could hitchhike to a nearby city and start her life over.

Again.

The idea made her weary, but she'd known her life would be this way when she ran from Mark. His arms extended long and his power was unstoppable. She'd do what she had to to stay alive and keep the people around her safe.

Stepping into the shower, Carey winced when the hot water ran over her scalp. She pressed her lips together and remained quiet, knowing Reilly was trying to sleep on the other side of that door. After all he had done, he deserved some rest and time away from her. She was grateful he'd kept his word and hadn't pressed to know more about Mark. Carey didn't have the energy to discuss him.

She turned in the shower, letting the hot water soothe her body. The shower felt heavenly. The tiles were snow white and the grout clean, the tub without sticky grunge coating the bottom, the water pressure perfect to massage her back muscles.

Taking a bottle of shampoo from the ledge, she poured some into her palm and worked it into a thick lather. The contact of the soap to her head stung and her rib cage protested the movements of her arms with pulses of pain. But it felt too good to be this clean, so she ignored her body's aches. Closing her eyes, she thought of Reilly, of the tenderness of his touch, the kindnesses he'd shown her. If she allowed herself and if her life had been different, falling for him would be easy.

No. She couldn't go there. Not now. Maybe not ever. Her life didn't allow her to play for keeps.

Ignoring the heaviness in her chest, she rinsed her hair and scrubbed her body quickly, lingering an extra few minutes beneath the hot water.

Carey turned off the water and stepped out of the tub, wrapping herself in the plush towel Reilly had given her. Even the towels here felt nicer than she'd had in her apartment. They were thick and smelled of fabric softener. After wiping her feet on the bath mat, she scampered to her room and closed the door.

Inside her duffel she had the one luxury she'd allowed herself to save from her old life—her lingerie. Carey rationalized no one except her would see it beneath the shapeless frump of her clothes. She'd tried to outwardly stifle her femininity, figuring a woman was an easier target for a mugging than a man. But she'd needed something to remind her she was a woman.

Sliding on her bra and panties, she tugged on her oversize jeans, using her belt to hold them around her waist. But when she reached her arms up to pull her navy-and-red-striped rugby shirt over her head, she muffled the scream that came to her lips. Pain shot down her spine, exploding across her arms.

She dropped the shirt and moved toward the bed. If she could lie down and stretch her back, she would be fine. She must have a pinched nerve or a torn muscle.

But she couldn't bring herself to move. Every muscle twitch was utterly painful. What should she do? Call out for help? She was standing in Reilly's bedroom in her jeans and bra. How embarrassing was this?

She heard movement in Reilly's bedroom. Was he awake?

"Reilly?" she called, keeping her voice low. If he didn't respond to her summons, she would assume he was sleeping and try Plan B. Okay, she didn't have a Plan B, but she would figure something out. Her mantra played through her mind. "Take it one minute at a time."

"Carey?" his gruff voice answered back.

Grimacing, she spoke. "Umm, I got a little problem."

The door to her bedroom banged open in seconds. He swore under his breath at the sight of her bruised body and then averted his eyes. "Why didn't you tell me you were hurt this badly?"

She was utterly aware she made an appalling sight with her baggy, worn jeans, bruised body and ratty, uncombed red hair. The dark red hair dye had been on sale at the drugstore and after several washings had turned brighter, like the color of Pebbles Flintstone's hair—not her intention. Yeah. She was a train wreck. Her humiliation spread from the root of her hair to her toes. "You knew about some of it," she said lamely.

His eyes glimmered with concern. "What's wrong?"

It took her a few moments to process his question. Reilly had stripped out of his dress shirt and tie and had been sleeping in a tight black T-shirt that made it obvious she'd been right about the muscles beneath his clothes. Roped arms, steely chest, tight abs. *Yowsa.* "My back. I can't move without shooting pain up my spine."

He held out his hands in a calming gesture. "Okay, just take it easy. Can I come closer?"

Yes. For heaven's sake, yes. Although if he touched her, the fierce need pooling in her stomach might ignite and consume her. "Sure."

Reilly kept his eyes riveted on her face and an odd sensation of delight roiled through her. Perhaps it wasn't disgust at her bruises. Maybe this was his way of showing respect for her in her awkward, half-naked form. That thought strengthened her desire. What she needed was for him to do something appalling to turn her off.

Reilly held his hands a few inches from her body. "I'm going to see if you have anything broken, okay?"

"My rib cage hurts pretty badly," she said. "And my back hurts when I move."

He set his hand along her spine and then touched her rib cage. Pain shot to her side, followed by excited sparks at the contact.

"Your ribs might be broken or bruised."

Carey took a deep breath and winced. Even that hurt. "Can I get some more pain medication?" Aspirin. Ibuprofen. Anything.

"My father was a medic for the SEALs. Can I have him examine you?"

"Could I get something to wear? Or maybe a blanket?" It was uncomfortable enough being with Reilly half-naked, never mind in front of his father. Reilly thought for a moment. "Let me get you a zip-up sweatshirt. We can put it on without too much movement."

Almost before she could blink, he'd returned with a sweatshirt. He slipped it over her arms and zipped the front. "Better?"

Marginally. "Thank you. I don't feel comfortable with…"

"No worries. I understand."

An unexpected connection zipped between them. She didn't have to explain or put words to how she was feeling. He got it. He got *her*.

Reilly left and returned a few minutes later with his father, who introduced himself as Doc. He had the kindest eyes she'd ever seen and much like with Reilly, she instinctively trusted him—as least a little bit. She'd made some pretty bad decisions in the past. The latest incident with the Vagabond Killer in the alley was a great example.

"How did you come by these injuries?" Doc asked.

He stated the question casually, but she heard something clinging to the edge of his words. How should she answer? Did Reilly want him to know the truth? She shot Reilly a questioning look, and he nodded at her to continue.

Minimal information was best. "Yesterday I walked into a situation. A fight in an alley. I tried to blast the guy with pepper spray, which made him pretty mad."

Doc looked at his son, his brow furrowed. "You weren't with her?"

Reilly shook his head. "I was working."

Doc harrumphed. He held the hem of the sweatshirt she wore in his hand. "May I?" he asked and she nodded. He lifted the shirt slightly and examined her rib cage. "Best guess is you have some bruised ribs."

Her streak of bad luck continued. "What can I do?"

"You should see a doctor and get some X-rays. See if there's other damage," Doc said.

Slow breath in, slow breath out. "I can't do that."

"Why not?" Doc and Reilly asked at the same time.

Myriad reasons. She didn't have a real identity or health insurance. If she admitted she didn't have the money, Reilly might offer to pay and she owed him too much already. "I want to wait a few days and see if it heals itself." Was that possible?

Doc twisted his lips in thought, but mercifully, didn't argue. "Then we'll keep them wrapped and try not to jostle you too much. Let's get some aspirin for the pain."

Reilly and his father set about getting her medication and wrapping her rib cage with some ACE bandages. Then Reilly lifted her, moving her as little as possible, and laid her on the bed. "You need to rest your body. Try to let your muscles relax."

"Let me know if it gets worse," Doc said. "And Reilly, watch out for your woman from now on. I raised you better."

"I'm not his woman," Carey said, staring at the ceiling. She couldn't let Reilly's family go on thinking he had been negligent somehow. He was wonderful. Attentive. Thoughtful. She was the one who brought trouble everywhere she went. If she didn't leave soon, she might bring it here.

Doc coughed. "Oh, my apologies. I misunderstood."

She couldn't see his face, but his voice was lighthearted, as if he knew different.

Doc closed the door behind him, leaving Reilly and her alone.

"Can I do anything for you?" Reilly asked, sitting at the foot of the single bed, widening the space between them. Was he doing it on purpose? He *had* to feel it, too, the skin-tingling awareness of each other.

He could do plenty of things for her. Hold her. Tell her everything would be all right. If he spoke the words, she would pretend to believe them for a short time. Shoving aside her ridiculous wish, she made a more practical request. "Could you help me brush my hair? It hurts to move my arms above my head and my hair will look like a real rat's nest if I don't brush it."

"I can do that," Reilly said.

It had been difficult to ignore her attraction to him when he'd been dressed like a detective. In the black T-shirt, it was impossible. Too easy to forget what he did for a living and see him as a man. A strong, virile man. "My brush is in my duffel," she said, trying not to stare at the sleek movement of his muscles beneath his shirt.

Reilly collected it and helped her sit up, letting her back rest against a mound of pillows. Being on the bed together, close enough to touch, added fuel to an already raging fire.

"This is an interesting choice of colors," he said.

Casual conversation. Sure. She could do that. "You don't think the red is natural?" she asked wryly.

He chuckled. "Not for a minute." He took a section of hair and worked the brush through it. "Tell me if I hurt you. I'll try to be careful, but I can't say I've ever done this."

His hands brushed over her, the most delicate of

touches. She closed her eyes against the sensation. "I'll let you know. My hair is blond."

"Not many natural blondes left in the world," he said.

Her pulse beat faster at the simple caress of his hands moving through her hair. "I'm lucky that way, I guess," she said.

Given her current situation, she'd meant it as a joke, but Reilly didn't laugh. He pulled the brush down a long plait of her hair. "You have beautiful hair."

He could affect her so effortlessly. "Surely you jest," she said. The color was hideous.

"The color is a little out there, but it's soft." He was careful around the cut on her head. The rounded tips of the brush stroked her scalp, and the gentleness was a treat she hadn't had in months.

A moan escaped her lips. "That feels good." Her muscles unwound and her nerves came down a few notches.

He continued around her head, moving the brush in long, slow strokes. "I'm glad I could help."

There it was again. That feeling deep in her gut, something that clamored at her to get closer to this man, to grab on to him and not let go. He was kind and gentle; he was strong and sexy. She ached to reach out and touch him.

Forgetting about the pain, she leaned closer. "Reilly."

The word was spoken like a plea—*kiss me, please kiss me.* It had been a long time since she'd been with a man and even longer since she'd been with a good man. Reilly and his family were good people. It was plain to see in the manner they lived, how they spoke to each other and how they'd welcomed her, a perfect stranger, into their home.

"Yeah?" he asked, his expression closed.

She didn't have long to stay and she shouldn't start

something, especially when he'd pulled away twice already, but she couldn't stop herself. "Kiss me."

He stilled. "I don't think that's a good idea."

The rejection stung but didn't stop the need. "Kiss me."

"Carey," he protested, only halfheartedly.

"One kiss. One innocent kiss. It's been so long and I..."

"You what?" he asked, his eyes searching her face.

Wanted him. Couldn't pretend otherwise. "Need you to kiss me."

His eyes darkened and when he surrendered, his mouth capturing hers, the kiss was anything but innocent. Carnal, raw, hungry, his tongue invading her mouth, flicking along her lips, devouring her. She set her hands on his thighs, stroking him with her fingers, letting him know how much she loved what his mouth was doing to her.

His arms closed around her, shifting her onto his lap. A small cry escaped her lips at the move. She muted it, not wanting him to stop. He tried to pull his lips away, perhaps to apologize, but she clamped her hand around the back of his head, holding him to her.

He tasted like mint and he smelled spicy, like a man, a real man.

He finally tore his mouth away. "We can't do this."

Still reeling from the impact of his kiss, anticipation throbbing in her body, she blinked in confusion. "Why? Why can't we?"

He shifted her back to the bed and came to his feet. "This isn't right. You're the witness in a case. And you're hurt."

Ignoring the pulse of pain in her side, she threw her legs over the edge of the bed. "I'm fine. Really. I know it's crazy, but I feel—" She didn't know how to finish that sentence. Alive? Excited? Overwhelmed?

Reilly ran a hand through his hair. "You need to rest."

Carey took a deep breath to control her racing heart. He felt *something*. That kiss had spoken loudly. "I know what I need."

"You're injured."

"I'm fine." Even putting emphasis on the word made her ribs burn.

"This isn't a good idea." He spoke the words with finality, but offered no further explanation. "Come into the bathroom and I'll bandage your arm," he said, the heat that had been in his face a moment before completely gone.

Chapter 5

The smell of baked chicken and stuffing wafted into the air making Reilly's mouth water.

"You and your friend are on the news," Reilly's mother announced as they sat down for dinner. Jane set the steaming dish she was carrying onto a trivet near the center of the table.

Reilly glanced at Carey sitting next to him, her face masked with a haunted expression. He couldn't tell if her back was that rigid because of her bound ribs or pure terror. Time to come clean. "Then you know Carey's not here for a visit. She's under my protection."

Reilly's older brother Harris took his seat at the table. "Your protection, our protection. Can someone pass the potatoes?"

Carey pushed herself away from the table, her plate empty and her lips drawn into a thin line. "Excuse me. I'm not feeling well. Maybe I should see a doctor tomorrow." Her voice shook with heavy emotion.

Reilly had seen that look in her eyes before. "Nice try. You're not running. I'm not driving you into town so you can take off at the first opportunity."

Carey pitched her gaze around the room. "I shouldn't be here. You don't have to put your family at risk because of me."

Reilly snorted. "We're not at risk. Let someone come here for you. They'll see the mistake they've made when they're greeted with the business end of my father's rifle."

The family chuckled, but Carey's face remained strained with worry. "Don't you want to know what I did?" she asked his mother.

"I saw the report. You witnessed an attempted murder." Jane spoke the words without emotion, without worry.

He'd let Carey fill in the details if she wanted. His family knew enough to know they needed to protect her.

"If you saw the report, so did the Vagabond Killer. He'll come looking for me," Carey said.

"We've talked about this," Reilly said, setting his hand on her arm. Her skin was soft beneath his fingertips and he drew away his hand, aware that touching her heightened the temptation. What was wrong with him? He couldn't stop touching her. As many times as he told himself she was off-limits, he didn't have the restraint he needed to keep his distance. Something about her decimated every last ounce of his control.

Carey scrubbed her hands over her face. "I know, but a part of me thought maybe they wouldn't run my picture or maybe the story would stay localized in Denver. If the news has made it to Montana, then it's probably all over the internet."

"Even if someone recognizes you, no one except the

ADA and the lieutenant knows where you are," Reilly said. "And I mean no one," he emphasized, driving home the point that the Vagabond Killer and the man Carey was running from were both in the dark. The thugs following them couldn't have guessed their final destination. The Truman Ranch was not on any official radar.

Harris set down his fork. "The Vagabond Killer won't leave the city searching for her. At least not yet. It'll take his psyche some time to work up the nerve to leaving his hunting ground. Serial killers have a pattern of behavior. As deranged as they are, their killings and stalker tendencies aren't usually random."

Jane set her hand over Harris's and squeezed. "Even if someone is searching for her, they won't think to look here."

Harris smiled apologetically. "Sorry. Wasn't trying to be a killjoy. Profiler training—it pops out at the worst moments."

No one's words seemed to ease her worry.

Carey bit her lip. "It's a matter of time before he finds me. I have to get out of here. Vanessa or the lieutenant could let something slip."

"If anyone comes here, we're ready," Doc said. "Can you pass the butter?"

Carey remained quiet for a moment as if considering the situation and handed Doc the white ceramic container of butter. Reilly watched her out of the corner of his eye. She appeared confused, then her face filled with disbelief. Anyone who hadn't grown up with a Navy SEAL father and a CIA agent mother didn't understand the security that came with his well-connected family. His mother wasn't a large woman, but if tested, she'd prove herself a valiant opponent. His father was outwardly calm, making it that much more unexpected when he sprang into action.

That Reilly and both of his brothers had gone into various fields of law enforcement and protection was no surprise to anyone who knew their family.

Carey rubbed her side and Reilly wondered if the pain medicine he'd given her was helping. "Every other officer on the force is required to work. Isn't it going to look strange when you're the only one missing and you were the one at the scene and in the picture?"

The thugs had also seen them together, but Reilly didn't point that out. He was impressed she had caught onto a detail that small. "I'm not officially on leave, and I'm planning to show up in the precinct every few days. If anyone knows you're with me, they'll assume I dropped you off somewhere."

She shook her head as if trying to understand. "Being connected to me puts you at even greater risk."

Reilly didn't see it that way. He'd taken this assignment because he could do it well. He would protect Carey. "I'll be fine." He'd be extra-vigilant and on guard for an attack while he was away from the ranch. On the off chance the man stalking Carey approached him, he'd be ready.

"You're going to drive eight hours each way to keep the cover?" Carey asked.

Harris snickered. "If you knew the kinds of bull this family has done to keep someone's cover, you wouldn't think driving eight hours is that big of a deal. We once ran an obit for Dad's death and had a baby announcement printed for our 'new sister' to explain Mom's leave of absence from her job." Harris made finger quotes around the words *new sister*.

Reilly would drive a hundred times that distance if it

meant keeping Carey safe. "It's not a problem. A jug of coffee for the drive and showing up at a couple of key places in the city should do it," Reilly said. "Cop bar, twenty-four-hour diner, that sort of thing."

"You'll stay on the ranch," Doc said. "We'll get whatever you need. No one will know you're here. I'll order more surveillance equipment and keep the alarms on every entrance to the house."

Reilly appreciated every member of his family stepping up to reassure her. When her pained expression remained, Reilly jumped to console her. "It's not forever. A few days, maybe a few weeks. We're going to catch the Vagabond Killer."

She stared blankly at her plate and he knew she was thinking about the man she was running from. Reilly swore to himself that if he ever found the man who was terrorizing her, he'd see to it he paid for his crimes. As little as he knew about Carey, he knew she didn't deserve to live in fear. She deserved happiness and a chance at a real future. "You'll have your life back."

The look she gave him made it clear she'd caught his intended meaning.

"If it makes you feel better, I'll show you my gun locker," Doc said. "Or our safe house inside the barn."

"Ha. Dad wants to show off his toys," Harris said with a grin.

The beginnings of a smile lit Carey's face. "I'll take your word for it. Guns make me nervous and I hope we never need to hide in a safe house."

Jane waved her hands to get everyone's attention. "Let's not spoil dinner with the incessant guns, ammo, and doomsday talk."

"It's a family favorite though," Harris said.

"You know what else is a family favorite? Stories of

you boys when you were young. Perhaps Carey would like to hear about which of you wore diapers the longest and how Reilly refused to eat anything except carrots for a week and turned orange."

Harris and Reilly held up their hands in mock surrender.

"You win, Mom. Point taken," Reilly said, reaching for Carey's hand and giving her a squeeze. The action came so naturally, he wasn't aware he'd done it until he felt her stiffen and the eyes of his family bearing down on him.

He pulled his hand away and set it on his fork. He had to stop touching her.

Witness, he told himself. She was a witness to a crime. She wasn't his to comfort. His job was to keep her safe so she could do a lineup and then testify after they'd caught the Vagabond Killer. He couldn't lose objectivity, and that was precisely what would happen if they got involved.

Carey paused when Reilly's hand touched hers. The first two times he'd touched her at dinner, she'd brushed the contact aside as casual. But the third time, it started to feel deliberate. Never had a man's hand felt so warm, so encompassing. He was commanding, capable and protective. And she, no doubt, had brought out the fiercest guardian in him. She'd been secretive about her past and she was involved in tracking a serial killer. She had "pile of mess" written all over her.

Yeah, Reilly Truman definitely thought he'd struck White Knight gold when he'd found her. She had problems and he was a troubleshooter.

The Trumans could too easily lure her into a false sense of security. They were nice people, who appeared genuinely interested in helping her, but everyone had their price. Her father had proven that, Mark had proven that and her mother had proven that. For the right dollar amount, a person would do anything.

Mark had plenty of dollars to use for convincing, which was why Carey had to break free before he tracked her here, before he found her living with the Trumans. The Trumans didn't deserve to be pulled into her messy life. They'd be collateral damage and she'd never forgive herself. Mark already had two of his men trying to track her down, probably more.

Reilly passed her a plate of chicken, and despite her stomach twisting in worry, she took a small piece from the platter.

When had she last been offered a home-cooked meal? She might as well eat until she was full. Carey took a forkful of chicken. She'd been eating mechanically for eleven months, usually peanut butter and bread or a cup of ramen noodles, and she was unprepared for her taste buds' reaction to fresh food.

She let out a moan and quickly took another bite.

Jane smiled at her. "I'm glad you like my food. My family wolfs theirs down so fast, I never get compliments."

"Asking for thirds *is* a compliment," Reilly said and took another bite of potatoes.

Carey's face heated. "I'm sorry. It's been a long time since I've eaten anything home-cooked."

"You don't cook?" Jane asked.

Sadly, she didn't have the chance. "I don't have a kitchen in my apartment," she said. For a brief moment she worried she'd given away too much. Reilly had seen her apartment though, so she hadn't given anything away he didn't already know. But she had to be more careful. A few hours with the Trumans, one thoroughly arousing kiss, and several of Reilly's heated touches, and she was spilling details about her life. Big mistake.

Doc's brows furrowed. "I thought you were a little skinny. Not enough protein. When you return to the city, Reilly will make you a meal fit for a king. Or queen."

Carey expected Reilly to protest. Instead he chewed and nodded at her. He swallowed and took a sip of water. "My dad's not kidding. I love to cook. My work schedule means dinner is sometimes at midnight, but I don't mind."

For one minute she let herself buy this fantasy, that she was actually returning to the city with Reilly and they'd have a friendship of some sort. Or the chance to explore the persistent attraction between them. "I don't get off work until midnight, either." Where was the filter over her mouth? Again, Reilly probably knew she worked late based on the time of the crime, but still…

"Perfect," Jane said, her eyes shining as she looked between her son and Carey.

Carey knew that look. It was a mom look, one that said she wanted to know more about the relationship between her son and the woman at his side. It was the same look Mark's mother had given her when they'd met. At the time, Mark's mom had wanted an in to the lifestyle that organized crime afforded—great parties, fancy clothes, expensive jewelry. Carey had been her ticket into that life and Mark's ticket to the head of it. Carey shivered. She hadn't seen it coming.

"Are you cold?" Reilly asked.

Carey brought her attention back to the table conversation. "Sorry, my mind drifted."

"What do you do for a living?" Doc asked.

"I work at a Laundromat," Carey said, checking

every word. She couldn't tell them any more than Reilly already knew.

Harris hit the top of the table. "Match made in heaven. Reilly can't understand the difference between a light load and a dark load. You can show him."

"I do understand the difference, I just don't have time to bother," Reilly grumbled with a small smile on his face.

"When we lived at home, no one would let him touch their laundry. If one of my socks got mixed in with his stuff, it came back pink or grey. Terrible," Harris said, shaking his head.

Jane interrupted. "Carey, I don't want you to think I didn't raise my sons to know how to take care of themselves."

"This is why I never bring women around," Reilly said, grinning at his family. "You guys love to embarrass me, like by telling how I turned orange and turned my socks pink."

Reilly volleyed back a few bombs on his family in return. Watching them, listening to their teasing, she felt like an outsider intruding on a place she didn't belong. This was the family she'd wished she'd had. Laughter. Smiles. Jokes.

Nothing like her own.

Sitting with Reilly and his family, loneliness descended. She'd never have this life. The ache in her chest intensified. The sooner she left the better. Not only would the Trumans be safer, she wouldn't have the reminder of what she'd never have.

"I'll run out to the woodpile and grab a few logs for the fire," Reilly said, shrugging into his jacket.

"Do you want help?" Harris asked.

Reilly shook his head. "Nah, I can handle it." A few pieces of wood were all they needed to have a fire in the hearth for the evening. He trudged out the back door into the cold to the chopped woodpile on the porch. What else could he do to make Carey feel more secure? He could sense her fear and her distance, as if she were holding herself back. Their family banter and attempts to reassure her hadn't calmed her.

His cell phone vibrated in his pocket. Pulling it out, he glanced at the display. Unknown number. It could be Vanessa or the lieutenant calling with an update on the case. He answered, "Truman."

"Detective Truman, how wonderful to speak to you."

Reilly's stomach torqued too tight, the same gut reaction he had whenever something was about to go very, very wrong. "Who is this?" He was grateful the phone was department issued and untraceable. Using his credit card had given away too much as it was.

"I'm the man who's been looking for your witness. I saw the two of you on the news today and it's been far too long since she and I have chatted."

Not the Vagabond Killer. This was the man Carey feared. Anger swelled in Reilly's chest and he tamped it down, fighting for control of his temper. "If you come near her, if you attempt to touch her, you will regret making such a bad decision."

The man had the audacity to laugh. "You have no idea who you're up against. Don't threaten me. Tell me where she is and no one will get hurt. I'll make it worth your while. Name your price."

Reilly couldn't be bought. Everything in him rejected the notion of accepting a bribe. "Even if I knew, I wouldn't tell you." He'd give this scum nothing to go on.

"Reconsider. I know you left Denver. It was an inconvenience to have two of my men questioned by the police, thanks to your call. I don't want to be inconvenienced again in this silly cat-and-mouse game. Bring her to the city, anywhere— You can even pick the place. I'd hate to see someone you care for hurt over such a silly thing as protecting a runaway."

"Leave her alone," Reilly said. He'd give nothing away, and the longer they spoke the more words this scum had to analyze looking for clues about Carey's location. He disconnected the phone.

Reilly slid his phone into his pocket. He'd call this into the DPD and see if they could run a trace *post facto* or get any information about the number who had called him.

Two psychopaths were after Carey. She had been right not to be lured into a sense of safety.

Carey couldn't draw a full breath. Mark had contacted Reilly. How long before Mark traced her to the Trumans' ranch using property records? For a few hours, she had been comfortable. She had believed she'd be safe.

She knew better. She wasn't safe anywhere. She was a risk to anyone with her.

"He wanted to know where Carey was hiding. He doesn't know where she is," Reilly said, taking a seat the kitchen table. "He's bluffing about his reach."

Cold fear froze Carey's insides. "Yet. He doesn't know where I am yet. It's only a matter of time until he tracks us here."

Jane shook her head. "We have this place registered under a false company name, and that company name isn't associated with us directly."

Harris drummed his fingers on the table. "It's pretty bold for the killer to call you."

Reilly hadn't told his family the call had come from Mark and not the Vagabond Killer. But Carey knew by the description of the voice and the words. Mark was arrogant and controlling. He expected to hand out tasks and for people to follow his instructions.

Doc stood and retrieved a notebook from the counter. "He might assume Reilly escorted you to a safe house in Colorado. Using a detective's personal connections to house a witness is unusual. You're safest here. Going on the run and looking for another place to stay puts you on the defensive. Better to work on the offensive. If someone comes here, we'll be ready. We won't take chances. We'll schedule patrols during the day and keep our eyes and ears open. No one will make it onto the premises without our knowledge."

As the family discussed options to ensure her safety, contingency plans, and additional protections, Carey watched, not able to keep up with the conversation. The Trumans were going to disrupt their lives and their holiday for her. They were putting themselves at risk. Mark wouldn't hesitate to hurt someone to get to her.

Carey looked at her feet. It wasn't right other people should suffer because of her decisions. "I never meant to drag anyone into this. This is my problem. Maybe I should go."

Reilly came to his feet and then knelt in front of her. She met his gaze and their high-voltage connection charged through her. Excessive energy and longing escalated in her body. A sense of connection, a rightness with him tempted her to open up and share the part of her life she'd been running from for months. If only she could tell him and not risk his life, she'd make room for him inside her heart. Their physical attraction could be so much more. If only.

"I don't want to hear any more talk of you running again. I was assigned to protect you and I'm going to keep you safe," Reilly said.

The surge of excitement from his nearness was immediately replaced with a chill of fear. She didn't know if anyone was strong enough to protect her from Mark.

Carey sat perched on the edge of the couch, watching Reilly play with the fire in the hearth. He added another log to the roaring blaze. After talking for a few minutes in the family room, the Trumans had left her and Reilly alone, each making excuses about chores and plans they had after dinner.

Should she make an excuse and go to bed, as well? A heightened sense of anticipation clung to the air. Did Reilly want to talk to her about the case? Pry for more information about her past? Discuss Mark's phone call?

Closing the screen around the fire to catch the sparks of ash, Reilly took a seat on the floor. The firelight flickered across his face, the warm glow illuminating the room. The smell of wood burning brought back memories of summer camp and cold winter nights curled on the couch with a blanket and a book. Comforting memories.

"How are you holding up?" Reilly asked.

She sensed he wanted to ask questions and was holding back. Because of the promise he had made not to dig?

She touched her side. "My ribs are still a little sore and my arm hurts if I move it a certain way. But dinner was great." At least until the point when Mark had delivered his threat. "It's been a long while since I've eaten that well."

Reilly smiled, making his handsome face even more beguiling. "My mom loves to cook. When she retired, she discovered entire television channels devoted to cooking and now it's her passion."

Carey focused her attention on the fire. It was dangerous to feel anything for him or to let her imagination play with possibilities. Even gratitude created dangerous connections. She couldn't think about Reilly. She had to focus on getting out of here. She couldn't stay here and wait for Mark to find her. The Trumans might have their ranch well hidden, but Mark had the resources and money to buy the information he wanted. "Your family has been wonderful to me."

Reilly set the poker on the bricks lining the hearth. "They're pretty great. What about your friends or family? Isn't someone wondering where you are?"

Carey slid to the floor, letting her back rest against the couch. She stretched her legs in front of her, her feet in reaching distance of Reilly. She should tell him in no uncertain terms she wasn't going to talk about her life. He'd promised he wouldn't press her about her past and she wasn't naïve. They couldn't share secrets. Their relationship needed boundaries. He was a detective, committed to working on the right side of the law, and she was the daughter of a crime lord. If she told him about her family and the things they had done, the crimes they'd committed, Reilly would look at her with disgust on his face. That was something she could live without. "You mean, is anyone looking for me besides two criminals?"

Compassion softened his face. "You're safe here, Carey. I'm going to take care of you."

Carey shifted. This was the reason she hadn't gotten close to anyone in the last eleven months. It created too many complications, like trusting someone, relying on them to help, opening up to them. Carey worried constantly that sharing something could get her or someone else killed.

Her father had trusted Mark with his life. Her father had bestowed his blessing on his only daughter to marry Mark, and then Mark had betrayed him.

Not that her father was an innocent who'd been forced into the life he'd led. In the endless hours of solitude, Carey had tried to resolve the logical side of her brain that understood her father was involved in a violent lifestyle and the emotional side of her brain that loved her father and couldn't imagine him doing harm to anyone.

"I don't want to talk about the case." At his nod of agreement, she continued. "I've been alone for a long time. I've gotten used to it," she said. A lie. She was numb to it at times, refusing to cry over her fate. But she wasn't used to it.

"How long have you been running?" Reilly asked.

She didn't want to give exact times. He was smart. He'd dig around until he could put the pieces together, missing persons who looked like her from a given time frame. "Longer than I thought possible. But now that I'm far away from that life, I realized, in one way or another, I've been alone most of my life."

Reilly inclined his head and remained quiet, his focus on her, encouraging her to continue. It felt good to talk to him, to talk to someone who wasn't trying to get something from her or use her to get closer to her father or Mark.

She could stick to the ancient past. Before Mark. That was safe. "My mother left us when I was two. She moved to Las Vegas to dance in a show on the strip. I definitely did not inherit her gracefulness. I took dance lessons once in high school and I bruised my partner's feet."

"Everyone's awkward as a teenager. I bet you're much better now. I bet you dance beautifully."

Carey clamped her mouth over her rebuttal. Mark had taken her to dance lessons in a rare display of romantic interest, in preparation for their wedding. More times than not, he had stormed out of class in frustration because she couldn't remember the steps, she didn't move in the right direction and she counted off beat.

Reilly reached for a remote sitting on the side table behind him. He pressed a few buttons and the speakers in the corners of the room piped soft holiday music. He came to his feet and extended his hand to her. "Dance with me. Please."

She frowned and shook her head, even as she found herself reaching for his hand. "A man who grew up in a house with music in the living room will put me to shame."

He pulled her upright, bringing her body close to his, his hips inches from her stomach. Every nerve ending in her body tingled in awareness.

"It's just you and me. No one will see."

Her heartbeat skipped, faltered.

He tucked her into the circle of his arms, holding her around the waist and clasping her left hand in his, pressing her hand to his chest. Reilly swayed slightly, his body in time with the music. "Just relax," he whispered. "Close your eyes and let me lead you."

His eyes were closed, so she shut hers and let his strong arms guide her. She was no Ginger Rogers, but at least she didn't step on his feet. He wasn't planted in one space, either. He moved, his hips brushing her body, his knee touching the inside of her thigh. Her skin prickled with sensation and her pulse scrambled to catch up with her racing heart.

He did the work and she was along for the ride. As Reilly moved, he hummed quietly, and she leaned closer to hear him, basking in the heat of his body. The deep timbre of his voice shivered along her spine and he adjusted his arms around her, closing the inches between them. Achy, hungry desire amplified inside her.

"Carey," he said, each syllable catching on the music.

Opening her eyes, she met his gaze and fell into her lust-charged emotions. The fire in his eyes matched the heat in his voice.

She'd let herself have this one song, just this one to blot out Mark and the Vagabond Killer, and then she'd jolt herself right back into reality. One song wouldn't cause any harm, would it?

Her body was completely turned over to him. She lifted her mouth, her lips parted in invitation. He wasn't any more immune to her than she was to him. She saw the kiss in his dark eyes before he lowered his head to deliver it. His lips fell onto hers, brushing, light, giving.

A deep, burning need sliced through her. He brushed his lips over hers, soft and unhurried. He stopped dancing and threw his complete attention to what they were doing, his lips sending shockwaves over her body, his kiss making promises she knew he couldn't keep. I'll protect you. I'll keep you safe. You're mine.

His hands reached into the back of her hair and angled her head to kiss her more deeply. She melted against him, her body to his, his arousal pressed into her stomach. The sensual slide of his hands urged her on, more, faster. She wanted to scream because what he was doing felt so amazing.

His hands moved to her sides. "Is this okay?" he asked, lifting his mouth slightly from hers.

"What?" she asked breathlessly, pressing her lips to his, desperate for his touch, wanting to savor every moment. How long had it been since she'd been in the warm embrace of a man? She knew for certain she'd never kissed a man like Reilly. It had never felt this way.

"Your ribs. Does it hurt when I touch you here?" he asked, brushing his hands down her back.

His touch ignited passion that flared in her belly, spreading to every part of her. "No, no, everything you're doing feels good."

He growled low in his throat, a sound echoing hunger. He walked backward to the couch and lowered himself, taking her with him, setting her legs over his hips so she was straddling him.

Kneeling over him, she cupped his face in her palms, lifting his head. She held his gaze and lost herself in his eyes. "You're a good man, Reilly Truman." He'd done what no other man had. He'd kept her safe, protected her, risked his safety for hers. When this was over, she wanted him to remember those words. They were the greatest truth she had spoken since she'd met him, no half-truth, no honesty hidden behind semantics. He was an impossibly honorable man—her head knew it and her heart feared it. She could too easily fall for him and trick herself into thinking she'd get a happily ever after.

Knowing this may be the only time they had together sent desperation and hunger spiraling in her veins. Carey ground her hips against his pelvis, the rough fabric of her jeans creating the perfect friction. He set his hands on her hips, sliding her along his hardness, lifting his hips and circling them against her.

Emotions bombarded her from every direction, tenderness, warmth and lust. Her eyelids grew heavy and the pressure between her legs tightened, higher, faster, more. "Reilly." She tightened her grip on his shoulders and let her head fall back.

He must have heard the plea in her voice, because he thrust harder against her, once, twice, excitement surging inside her, lifting her, shattering her. Blistering hot desire exploded in her body and she climaxed in his arms, her vision momentarily going sparkling white, waves of pleasure pulsing over her.

She slumped against him and he nuzzled the side of her neck.

The music hummed in the background, a soft, melodic tune, taking second to her roaring thoughts. The poignancy of the moment threatened to reach straight to her heart, touch her and irrevocably change her. She snuggled closer in his arms, loving the feeling of them banded around her and trying to put off thinking about the future. She wanted to linger in the now and pretend disaster wasn't waiting for her.

The song changed to a bright, vocal, upbeat piece. The mood broke and the haze of pleasure faded. Reality hit hard. Letting that happen with Reilly had been a mistake. She didn't need connections to him complicating her life, making it harder to run. When she left, she couldn't look back. For his sake she needed to put distance between them.

Reilly was the giver and she was the taker. He had put his life on the line to protect her and she was endangering him. He had asked her to dance and she'd been needy, hungry, begging him for more.

And he'd given, taking nothing for himself.

Her legs felt rubbery, but she managed to crawl out of his lap and onto the cushion next to him.

"Did I hurt you?" he asked, touching her thigh lightly.

And of course he would have to be sweet and concerned about her. "I'm fine."

"You say that a lot."

She didn't have a choice. If she let herself slip, if she started thinking about the bad things in her life, she'd crumble. She'd had her resolve set to "fine" for months. She reached over and set her hand on his arm, squeezing gently. "Most of the time, I am fine." She didn't want him to push too hard, or he could break through and see how scared she was beneath her fragile outer shell.

He opened his mouth and then snapped it shut.

"What? You can say whatever. It won't hurt my feelings," she said, shoring up her defenses. This was the life she led. The song was over and she had to let go of the fantasy. She was a woman on the run, and she would run as long as she had to to keep the people around her and herself safe.

"You're beautiful," he said.

No. Anything but more kind words. She wouldn't weaken. Chips in her armor could not be permitted. "But?"

He rested his head on the cushion of the couch. "No but. You're beautiful. I don't know what's going on in your mind, but I thought you should know what's going on in mine."

Carey's heart took flight and she wondered how much longer she could stay with Reilly and keep her boundaries in place.

Chapter 6

Reilly ran a shaky hand through his hair. Nothing rattled him. Not staring down the barrel of a gun, not confronting a perp. But this? It was like nothing he'd experienced. The raw passion had caught him off-guard and he couldn't afford mistakes now.

It was his job to protect her.

Why had he it let it go that far? Why hadn't he denied her that kiss? That kiss had opened a floodgate and with the water pouring out, it was impossible to stop.

Carey had escaped an abusive situation and was running from a man she believed would hurt her again. Instead of giving her space to think and clear her head, he'd gone and groped her like a teenager in a parked car.

A minute before, she was wild in his arms, and now she sat demurely, her knees pressed together. Another contradiction in her behavior. He guessed the real Carey was somewhere between the two women.

Carey needed him to be strong and steady. Reliable and nonthreatening. He wouldn't let this go further. He'd only meant to dance with her. She was vulnerable and scared and searching for some stability. Once they'd kissed, they'd both gone up in flames.

As a detective, he would do his job. As a man, he would keep his distance from now on. He wasn't interested in leading her on, knowing he couldn't get involved with her. She was the witness in a case. An important case. He'd seen firsthand what could happen when a detective became too close to a case. His former partner had lost his career, cast shadows of doubt over the department and ruined the integrity of an open-and-shut case. Reilly wouldn't make the same mistake.

Their flirtation ended tonight. No more kisses. No more fantasies of her writhing beneath him. "Are you ready for bed? It's getting late."

Carey jumped to her feet. "Bed? You want to go to bed?"

"I'll walk you to your room," he said, making it clear he wasn't propositioning her.

Reilly beat back the image of her astride him, her head thrown back, her red hair spilling over her shoulders. This ended here and now. He was stronger than that. More controlled. He was a Truman, and Truman men were disciplined and focused.

Lust exploded in his veins when she stopped at the entrance to the living room and turned to look at him over her shoulder. "It's dark. You lead the way."

It took everything he had to leave her in her room and walk to his alone.

Country breakfast took on a different meaning for Carey when seeing it in action in the Trumans' sprawling kitchen. It was a casual affair. Food choices lined the counters in dishes of varying shapes and sizes, and everyone grabbed a plate and served themselves buffet-style.

Reilly was the only member of the family missing from the kitchen and she was a little relieved he wasn't there. After escorting her to her room the night before and an awkward good-night, he'd gone to bed.

There were only two places left at the table—the same places where she and Reilly had sat for dinner. At least if she sat next to him, she wouldn't have to look across the table at him and wonder what he was thinking or if he was thinking anything about her. Or better, she could finish eating before he made an appearance.

She had other things to think about than Reilly and the dance they'd shared. A dance that had caught them in a whirlwind of passion. As much as she was drawn to Reilly, he and his family didn't deserve the pain and heartache she'd bring to their lives if she stayed too long. Mark would find her and he would hurt them. She couldn't allow that to happen.

"Do you want coffee?" Harris asked, breaking into her thoughts.

Carey focused on the conversation in the kitchen, her mouth watering at the smell of fresh-ground coffee wafting amidst the scents of bacon and sausage. "Yes, please."

Harris poured her a cup, handed it to her and nodded toward the sugar and creamer on the end of the table. Carey closed her eyes and inhaled, bringing the cup to her lips. It had been a long time since she'd had real, fresh coffee, instead of the swill they served at the convenience store across from her apartment.

She took a sip of the black liquid, letting it roll over her tongue and down her throat, warming her insides.

A shotgun blast shuddered against the windows and Carey jumped, dropping her coffee mug and splattering hot liquid on her sweatpants as she hit the ground and covered her head. The coffee mug shattered, spraying pieces of ceramic across the tiled kitchen floor.

They'd found her. Mark was already here.

Jane was at her side in a minute, stroking her back. "It's okay. We have hunters in the area."

Palms flat on the floor, Carey looked up at Jane and felt the penetrating gazes of Harris and Doc on her. Her face burned nearly as hot as the pain in her ribs and arm. The rest of the family was still in their seats, staring at her as if she had flipped off the Pope.

"I'm sorry for the mess," she mumbled, maneuvering to her knees.

Reilly chose that moment to enter the kitchen from outside, stomping his boots on the welcome mat set at the back door. Awareness arced between them. Assessing the situation with that focused look of his, his eyes locked on Carey crouched on the ground. She stood with trembling legs, her knees threatening to fold beneath her. Coffee was everywhere, some absorbed into her clothes and some splashed on the cabinets and floor.

"What happened?" he asked, looking between her and Jane in confusion. His gaze skipped down her body. Reilly wasn't just looking at the coffee stains. The sizzle and burn of forbidden attraction swept over her, raising her body temperature.

Jane answered for her. "A gunshot startled her. She's okay." Jane patted her shoulder.

Carey mentally thanked the Trumans for not making a big deal about this. She was embarrassed enough and, with Reilly's stare pinned on her, aware of how this must look.

"I should have warned you about hunters. It echoes out here with nothing to absorb the sound. They won't come on the property." Reilly's concern remained etched on his face. "I checked the grounds. There's no one on the ranch."

As tired as he had to be, he'd gotten up early to take a look around outside. Guilt swamped her, mingling with appreciation for what he'd done. For what they were doing to protect her.

"Let me get some paper towels to clean this up," Carey said.

Jane shook her head. "No, I've got this. You get yourself changed."

Carey looked down at her ruined clothes. Maybe she could put some soap on the brown marks and scrub them out. "Okay, that sounds good."

She fled upstairs and into her room, rummaging in her duffel for a dry pair of pants and another shapeless T-shirt. When she redressed, she opened the door to her room and found Reilly standing in the hallway waiting for her.

"Feel better?" he asked, crossing his arms over his chest. Something came into his eyes, a deep, sensual hunger. His biceps flexed and she recognized how sexy the stance was, how delicious he looked.

It took most of her focus to ignore it. "Yes, much. Do you think your mom will mind if I wash my clothes? At the rate I'm ruining them, I'll need a new wardrobe in a few days."

His gaze again wandered down her body, slower this time, steady, building heat in her chest with every passing second. "Wouldn't hurt."

His stare burned like a brand. "What wouldn't hurt?"

"Getting a new wardrobe."

Well then. Had she been imagining desire in place of scrutiny? Indignation had her lifting her chin. "What's wrong with my clothes?" She refused to mourn lost luxuries like expensive couture and leather handbags.

His appraisal swept over her. "Your clothes are too big and I know it's not because you find them comfortable."

Did he like what he saw? "How can you know what I find comfortable?"

Reilly stepped closer to her, the maleness of him nearly causing her to take a step back. Attraction sizzled and burned in the air between them. "I'm good at watching people. And I've been watching you quite a bit in the last two days. You dropped a *Vogue* magazine in the alley during the attack. CSI picked it up."

Carey had forgotten about the fashion magazine she'd had tucked beneath her sweatshirt. She'd read it at work on her breaks, both as an escape from her bland life and as a tool to keep anyone from talking to her. "I get the old ones free from the Dumpster." It ached to admit it. Yes, she had crawled into the Dumpster behind her building when she saw the shiny gloss of the magazine from her bedroom window.

If he was disgusted by her admission, it didn't show on his face. "You were looking at Vanessa's suit like you were dying to touch it," Reilly said, ticking the facts off on his hand.

Carey narrowed her eyes. "It was couture."

Reilly smiled smugly. "And my last and final proof that you'd much prefer something more feminine is that I saw you in your underwear."

The reminder wreaked havoc on her libido. Her pulse

beat erratically. She strove for indifference. "I'll take it as a compliment it made such an impression."

His eyes glimmered with heat and Carey's body overreacted the way it always did when he looked at her. "Oh, it made an impression. I've had that image, along with a few others, burned into my mind."

Forget indifference. She couldn't pull it off. "Like what?" she asked, her mouth feeling too dry.

His eyes filled with intense heat. "You dancing in my arms. Kissing you. You in my lap last night."

Longing singed her. Trying to understand Reilly was impossible. One moment he was shutting down, the next he was drawing her into a conversation about their relationship, making her feel hot and achy.

"Come on, Carey, we've got to talk about this thing between us. Ignoring it isn't working for me, and last night I went to bed with you on my skin, on my tongue, in my head. I had the most frustrating dreams about you."

A thrill of excitement swept over her. Confusion followed close on its heels. "You did?"

Reilly nodded once. "If we face it, the mystery is over and we can move past this."

A douse of cold water. Maybe he was right and she should scrub away any feelings she had for him. She'd known from the beginning this was a temporary situation. "What do you want me to say? We know this has an expiration date." The best they could have was a temporary, heated affair that would end when she ran.

"You seem to think everything in your life has an expiration date."

On some level, he had to understand why she thought in those terms. She wasn't letting herself imagine a future. She kept her response simple. "That's been the case."

Reilly shook his head. "You're selling yourself short. You could find a man, make a life with him and be happy."

His optimism stung. Not only was he being unrealistic, he'd drawn a line between them. Finding a man meant "not him." "I know my limits. I don't want to worry about the future."

"Is it so hard for you to believe that you could be happy? That you could have a future that doesn't include running?" Reilly asked.

Since the moment she'd decided to go on the run, she'd known she couldn't plan a future with Reilly or anyone else. Why then the disappointment spreading over her chest? On some level she had been letting herself fantasize about a connection with Reilly. "Experience tells me otherwise." Mark would pursue her. Relentlessly.

"I'm going to prove you wrong. You will have a future with someone," Reilly said. The quiet seriousness in his voice shook her.

Carey wouldn't let him convince her she had choices. That could only lead to more letdowns. "You can give it your best shot." She turned away before he could see the hurt on her face and question it. For a conversation he'd started to make the situation between them more clear, it had led to more confusion. She reaffirmed what she knew to be true—she had to run to keep herself and the people around her safe.

They returned to the kitchen and Carey filled her plate to heaping. Anxiety about her future, and disappointment that she'd left herself unguarded with Reilly, didn't curb her appetite, and eating gave her something to do besides avoid eye contact with Reilly. She sat at the table and then poured herself another cup of coffee. Jane had cleaned up the mess, and Carey carried her refilled mug with two hands, careful not to spill.

Harris turned on the television in the corner of the room, keeping the volume low. When his mother shot him a look, he shrugged. "I need my news fix. I want to know what's happening in the world."

Carey took a forkful of scrambled eggs, parts of her conversation with Reilly replaying in her mind. They hadn't resolved anything, except to clarify they were on different pages. Had she made the right decision by coming here with Reilly? Had she let things go too far? She was second-guessing every decision she'd made.

The TV news program flipped to Denver with an update on the Vagabond Killer case. Carey tensed. Would they show her picture, the one of her leaving the DPD, the one that had led Mark to connect her to Reilly?

"We're outside the Denver police station, where we've learned more about the measures the police are taking to track down the man known as the Vagabond Killer." The sketch she had helped create flashed on the screen. "A witness has come forward and provided this sketch of the suspect. Anyone with information is urged to the call the tip line, which is being manned twenty-four hours a day." An eight hundred number appeared at the bottom of the screen.

"Harris, please turn that off," Jane said. "We don't need to listen to that over breakfast."

Harris turned off the television, giving Carey an apologetic smile.

She'd been pretending the case was a world away. But she was naive to believe she'd escaped it. Curiosity getting the best of her, she finished her breakfast and retreated to Reilly's bedroom. Knowing she shouldn't, she turned on the small television on top of his dresser, switching the volume low.

Seeking news about the Vagabond Killer case wouldn't help her sleep better at night, but she had to know if the situation had changed.

She flipped the channel, and the face that appeared on the screen was more chilling than the Vagabond Killer's. Carey's hands shook so hard she dropped the remote.

Mark. Why was he on national television? Quieting the scream of terror in her mind, she stared at the screen.

As if speaking to her, Mark looked straight into the camera, his suit and tie crisp and clean. "We're committed to this merger that will make our winery the largest on the west coast, and we won't let anyone stand in our way. We have one legal issue we're close to eliminating and then it's full steam ahead."

Bile rose in Carey's throat. One legal issue. Eliminating. Meaning her. It was a thinly veiled threat.

Mark knew it was probable she'd be watching the news and no doubt had pulled strings to get the news of his business merger on TV. He'd found a way to terrorize her without having any direct contact with her.

Her time was limited. Mark would find a way to get to her. She'd been photographed with Reilly, and Mark had contacted Reilly looking for her. Was he digging into Reilly's background, searching for places she might be?

Terror tightened her throat and Carey fought the dizzying panic. Mark was going to find her. She had to leave. Where could she go? Was anywhere safe?

She checked her duffel bag again, needing the reassurance she was ready to run when she came up with a solid plan and found transportation to another city.

At the knock on her bedroom door, Carey scrambled to zip her duffel closed and turn off the television. She took a deep breath, trying to relax her face and shoulders to give the appearance nothing was wrong.

She pulled open the door. "Hi, Reilly." She tried for casual and missed the mark by a mile.

He inclined his head. "What's the matter?"

He had no doubt read her panicked expression. "Nothing." Nothing she was willing to discuss.

Reilly's eyes darkened, but he didn't press her further. "My mom is making Christmas cookies if you're interested in helping."

Making cookies beat hiding in Reilly's room and worrying. "That sounds fun."

Carey could pretend everything was fine. Especially when she was with the Truman family.

Over the next few days, each of the Truman men took turns patrolling the premises, and Harris and Doc had driven into town one morning to pick up extra camera equipment Doc had ordered. Reilly, Harris and Doc had set up the new equipment that afternoon.

The knot of fear in Carey's stomach had loosened. She couldn't hide forever, but for the first time in nearly a year, she didn't live with dread twisting in her gut every moment. Mark hadn't contacted Reilly again nor had he shown up at the ranch.

Carey lay in bed in Reilly's old bedroom for the fourth night in a row, staring at the ceiling. She hadn't come up with a safe plan to leave, in part because she didn't want to. She craved more time with the Trumans—their lively conversation, their easy manners and their acceptance of her, making her feel like part of their family.

And Reilly. He returned to her thoughts again and again. She sometimes caught herself watching him, loving to see him laugh, the gentle way he treated his family and his thoughtfulness with her. As many times as she reminded herself they couldn't have a future, it didn't stop her from thinking about how it would feel to kiss him again. Be held by him. Make love with him. She could handle a brief, steamy affair with him, couldn't she?

It was now or never. She couldn't stay much longer. Every moment she remained was another moment she risked bringing Mark to the Truman Ranch.

Carey rolled onto her side, pulling the thick blankets to her neck. She didn't want to leave. She was growing attached to Reilly and his family. But that was the reason she *had* to leave. Every moment she stayed with the Trumans increased the chances that Mark would find her.

Mark knew the last town where she had lived, and he'd find then scour her apartment for clues about her location. He would pay big money for information about her.

He stopped at nothing to punish those who betrayed him. And in his mind, she had betrayed him deeply. She'd run out on him the day of their wedding, escaping from the salon, the first chance she'd had away from him and his bodyguards in months. She'd sat at the pedicure station, her feet massaged by the bubbling water, and the moment the nail technician had closed the door to her private room, she'd pulled on her shoes, grabbed her handbag where she'd stuffed some essentials, popped the window open and run for her life.

Carey closed her eyes. She needed to get some sleep. Despite what the Truman family claimed, they weren't safe with her here. This could be the last good night's sleep she'd have for a long while. She snuggled under the covers, reveling in the soft feel of the sheets. Tonight, she wanted to dream of Reilly holding her and waking up beside her.

A car door slammed and her eyes flew open. She glanced at the clock radio on the bedside table— 3:00 a.m. God help them. This was no hunter. Mark had found her. She tore away the blankets and came to her feet.

Mark would arrive with a fleet of trained killers, and he would kill anyone who tried to protect her. Carey wouldn't let the Trumans come to her defense again and risk their lives to protect her. She couldn't escape Mark now, but she'd fight with everything she had and not let him hurt the Trumans. If she went outside, Mark didn't have a reason to come into this house and slaughter them while he looked for her. Carey tugged on a pair of sweatpants and grabbed an old baseball bat that Reilly had in the corner of his room.

It felt heavy in her trembling hand, her knees weak as she took the stairs to the main floor. She swallowed to keep the bile down and refused to lose her courage. She hefted the bat over her shoulder, gripping it with both hands. She'd meet Mark head-on, swinging and fighting like hell, screaming and making a ruckus, alerting the family and giving them time to protect themselves.

She barreled out the front door, shrieking with alarm, ignoring the blast of cold on her bare feet, and swung at the man coming up the stairs. He was not getting to the Truman family. She'd protect them with her life.

He let out his breath when the bat slammed into his

gut, the impact causing him to take a step down. It wasn't Mark, but it was no doubt one of his goons. She lifted the bat to strike him again and froze at the menacing look on his face.

His eyes narrowed in deliberate calculation and he disarmed her within seconds, tossing the bat over his shoulder. He snagged her around the waist, and she fought like a lioness, kicking at his shins, attempting to knee him between his legs.

Had the Truman family heard? Were they arming themselves or running for the safe house? Were there more men stationed around the perimeter of the house?

"For crying out loud, Brady, let Carey go."

Carey stopped thrashing at the sound of Reilly's voice and Brady turned her in his arms, setting her on the ground forcefully. She whirled to the porch where the Truman family stood watching her and Brady with perplexed expressions.

"Brady?" she asked, her stomach falling to her feet. "You're Reilly's brother?"

Brady rubbed his stomach, wincing. "Is this my welcome home party?"

Carey covered her face, mortified. She'd attacked Reilly's brother. Reilly came to her side, wrapping her in a blanket and lifting her off the ground. "What are you doing out here? You're going to get frostbite."

"I thought he was coming to attack us," Carey said, her mortification spreading bone deep.

Doc stood on the porch, an amused expression on his face. Jane was watching her and Reilly with interest, and Harris was howling with laughter. Only Brady looked furious. She was too embarrassed to meet Reilly's gaze.

"Never thought I'd see the day that Brady got his tail

kicked by a girl," Harris said, slapping his knee, barely able to remain standing upright.

"She caught me off-guard. I called Dad to tell him I was pulling in and he didn't mention we were keeping a wolverine for protection," Brady muttered.

"I'm s-sorry," Carey said. "I thought you wanted to kill me."

"Darlin', I don't even know you. Why would I want to kill you?" Brady asked. His slow drawl made it obvious he was more than a little irritated she had slugged him with a baseball bat. Carey's guilt went up a few notches. Everyone must think she was deranged.

"Why don't we go inside and talk about this?" Jane asked. "I'll make some tea and we'll catch Brady up."

Twenty minutes later, wearing Reilly's T-shirt, the blanket he'd wrapped around her, sweatpants and an oversize pair of Reilly's slippers, Carey sat next to him on the couch as he filled Brady in on the serial killer and the reason Carey was staying with them.

"What I don't understand is why she came barreling out of the house at me," Brady said.

Carey played with the edge of the blanket, rolling it between her fingers. "I figured if I attacked him first he wouldn't come into the house and hurt anyone else. It's me he wants."

"You thought if you attacked the Vagabond Killer, he would leave us alone?" Harris asked, his nostrils flaring.

Not the Vagabond Killer. Mark. But they didn't need to know that. The general principle was the same. "At the time, yes," she said. In retrospect, like the incident in the alley that had gotten her into this mess, it might not have been the best idea to go tearing after a would-be killer.

"What about you? If he was a murderer, he would have killed you," Reilly said.

Carey looked around at the equally intense faces of the Truman family. At least Brady looked less angry with her and more confused. "Maybe, but I had the bat—"

"Which I tossed to the ground in two seconds," Brady said.

"It was me who brought him here. I'm responsible," Carey said, pointing to her chest insistently.

"So it was a suicide mission," Reilly said.

She glared at him. "I made a split-second decision. I tried to help. These things don't always turn out how I hope."

Reilly came to his feet and paced. "What's his name?"

Carey took a sip of the tea Jane had prepared. It was harder to lie to him now than when she'd first met him. "I don't know. I just saw his face." He was calling her out. She heard it in his voice. Her reaction to Brady coming home tonight was the final straw. He wasn't taking any more vague responses to his questions. He wanted Mark's name.

"Not the Vagabond Killer. The man you're running from," Reilly said.

No one else spoke a word. "I told you I don't want to discuss the past. I think it's better if I leave. I don't want to get into this."

Reilly whirled. "Like hell."

"Reilly, calm down. You're scaring her," Jane said.

"You have more than one criminal after you?" Harris asked, lifting his eyebrow.

Carey looked at her lap, her eyes brimming with shame and tears. "Yes."

"I think now would be a good time for you to tell us about him," Reilly said through gritted teeth.

"I can't." She folded her hands around her cup of tea in her lap, fighting the tears of frustration that pooled behind her eyes. Reilly and his family wanted to help, but they couldn't. Mark was beyond the law. He was untouchable.

"What is it about him that scares you? Is he wealthy? Famous?" Harris asked.

Carey looked at Reilly, feeling betrayed he'd brought this up again. Why didn't he understand she was protecting them? "He has money." There. She'd answered.

"How do you know he's looking for you?" Jane asked, concern dotting her words.

Carey bit her lip. She didn't want this to turn into a guessing game where the Truman family slowly unraveled her secrets and exposed Mark's identity. "I'm sorry that I attacked Brady. It was an accident. I appreciate everything you've done." She let her eyes wander around the room, landing on the face of each Truman. Her throat grew uncomfortably tight. She came to her feet. She could pack and be out of the house in ten minutes. "It's best if I leave before anyone else gets hurt."

The family exchanged looks, communicating silently with one another. Reilly spoke for them. "If you aren't ready to tell us the whole story, we'll accept it. For now. But you're mine—that is, ours—to keep safe. You're not leaving here until we're sure you're going to be okay."

She nodded, knowing if she spoke, the tears she struggled to contain would break free. This family owed her nothing and yet here they were, giving her their loyalty.

"Why don't we leave them alone to talk this over?" Doc suggested.

The family murmured their agreement and all except Reilly filed out of the room one by one, Jane stopping to hug Carey good-night. Reilly stood with his feet braced apart, watching her.

"What can I say?" Carey asked, a tear slipping down her cheek. She wiped it away with the heel of her hand. Tonight accented the fact that she had stayed too long. Mark could have found her. Mark could have hurt the Trumans.

When he spoke, his voice was gentle. "I want you to tell me the truth."

Her heart ached. "I can't."

"Can't? Or won't?"

He was making this impossible. Couldn't he see she was doing her best to keep herself and his family safe? "A little of both."

"What are you afraid is going to happen? This ranch is one of the safest places for you to be right now. No one will find you here. I won't let anything happen to you."

Half of her fear was Mark finding her here, hurting her or the Trumans. As difficult as it was to admit, the other half was her fear that Reilly would despise her if he knew the truth about her life before she went on the run. The man she'd almost married was a career criminal. Her father had died after living a life of crime. A friend had died because of her. Compared to the Trumans, her family was terribly selfish. "I know you want to help me. And I know you need me to identify the Vagabond Killer. But I gave you the sketch. That's really all you need. I'll give a written testimony and I'll keep my eye on the news. When you've caught him, I'll contact you."

Reilly snorted. "I'm not that naive. Once you're in the wind, we'll never find you again."

Carey tapped her heel against the floor. Reilly wasn't that easy to convince. "Can't you see that I'm doing this for you? Because I care about you and your family?"

Reilly stepped closer, extending his hand and taking her by the elbow. "Promise me you'll stay for a little while longer. Give yourself a chance at a future that doesn't including running." His voice was low and thick.

The contact was electric, and his strong hand on her arm made her feel secure. Getting used to his protection was a mistake. She wouldn't have it for long. Lifting her head, she met his gaze and was temporarily mesmerized by the heat blazing in his eyes. Lying to him wasn't an option. He'd see through her. "How long is a little while?"

Reilly closed the distance between them. He removed the teacup from her fingers, set it on the coffee table, and then took her hands. "Until I say." He brought her hand to his chest and rested it there, freeing his and encircling her waist. His touch unhinged her and the last of her resistance crumbled away.

She lifted her head, offering him her mouth. He brought his down and brushed his lips across hers. There. She needed this, the physical comfort of Reilly's touch. The air around them crackled with emotion. She closed her eyes and waited for him to deepen the kiss.

Instead, he pulled away.

"What's wrong?" she asked, surprised at how breathless his kiss had left her.

He raked a hand through his hair and took a step back from her. "I can't figure you out. I don't know which of you is the real Carey."

For a brief moment, she nearly corrected him with her real name. It felt odd to think about her real name.

For so long, she kept that part of her buried, tucked away from the life she led now. "I'm always real."

"You fought a serial killer to help a stranger. You worked with a sketch artist when you could have run. Baseball bat aside, you're sweet to my family and yet you don't trust us. You close yourself off. You don't let anyone inside. Tell me who you are and let me see the real Carey."

She wouldn't let his kiss or his touch persuade her. Safety, hers and the Trumans', was her first priority. "I told you. I can't. And you agreed you wouldn't press me."

A muscle worked in his jaw. "I agreed I wouldn't press you about the past. I want to know who you *are*. Present."

A technicality. "I'm sorry, Reilly. I can't tell you anything more than I have." Her heart nearly shattered to speak the words. They drew a thick and heavy line between them, the distance lengthening with every utterance. She wanted to draw him closer and she wanted to keep him safe, a complete contradiction.

"Then I'm sorry, too. Because if you stopped running from everyone for a minute, you might find that you could actually be happy."

Chapter 7

Despite the late night, Reilly made the trip to Denver early the next morning and arrived midafternoon. He flashed his badge at the uniformed police officer who stood guard at the entrance of the DPD. Inside the squad room, chaos ruled. Volunteers and police officers working the phones sat at long tables, telephone and computer cords spilling to the floor. Information from each call was being recorded into a central computer system and analysts were reviewing the data and looking for commonalities that might lead to the Vagabond Killer's capture.

Every desk in the squad room was occupied, some with more than a few officers clustered around, reviewing data and discussing the case. The conference rooms were filled with men and women in suits, whiteboards displaying names and faces of victims. The team from the PR department was standing in the back of one of the conference rooms, taking notes and conferring among themselves.

"We're doing our best to keep the media out of the thick of this," Vanessa said over her shoulder to Reilly, weaving through the crowd toward the lieutenant's office.

"How's that working out?" Reilly said, knowing the media was still finding ways to get information. On the eight-hour drive from Ashland to Denver, nearly every station on the radio had mentioned the case.

Vanessa smirked. "Over a thousand people are working on this case in some capacity. How easy do you think it is to plug the leaks?" She reached the lieutenant's office and went inside, closing the door behind her, blocking some of the noise.

"I know how it works. People love to talk," he said. In some cases, the more people talked the better. But in this instance, as protective as he felt toward Carey, he wished the case hadn't hit the front page.

"How's the witness?" Vanessa asked, taking a seat behind the lieutenant's desk.

"She's hanging in," Reilly said. At least Carey hadn't bolted. Yet. She understood the severity of the case and her role. But she was also worried about the attention she was drawing, both from the Vagabond Killer and the man she was running from. Reilly curled and released his fists. Every time he thought of that man, quiet rage hummed inside him.

"What's on your agenda for today?" Vanessa asked.

Get the job done as quickly as possible so he could return to the ranch. "I'm going to make sure I'm seen around town. If anyone's connected me to the case from that picture, they won't see Carey with me and it might send them down a different path to find her." And if the man she feared was watching, he'd see that Reilly didn't give in to threats. Reilly wasn't bringing Carey to Denver until he was ready, and even then, no one was getting close enough to hurt her.

Vanessa nodded. "Not a bad idea. My office has received a few calls about protection assigned to the witness and some have asked us to confirm you're the detective overseeing her security."

"I assume they get a broad 'no comment' in response?" Reilly asked.

Vanessa smiled at him and folded her hands on the desk. "Exactly. You know how it works. We're going to get this guy. We have too many people looking. Someone is going to find something."

"The sooner the better." If they had the Vagabond Killer in custody and the lineup out of the way, he and Carey could focus on other problems. Like dealing with her past. Carey would confide in him eventually and once Reilly knew the identity of man she was afraid of, he'd make sure he never harmed her again. By the time she needed to testify, Carey would have no fear of anyone hurting her and could think about her future. He and Carey could move on with their lives.

Reilly's thoughts drew to a halt. When he pictured him and Carey moving on, he didn't picture them moving on separately. The image of them together, having dinner, watching television curled on his couch, spilled into his mind, followed quickly by the image of kissing her.

Kissing her until she was breathless and then taking her to his bedroom and making pulse-hammeringly slow love to her.

He jerked his mind out of the fantasy. He was in charge of her protection and he couldn't blur the lines between personal feelings and duty. This case was too critical to allow a personal mistake to ruin it. Any impropriety on his part could be shaded to appear as though he'd done something wrong—coached Carey or coerced her to lie. What happened to his former partner wouldn't happen to him and this case.

"We're lucky no one has figured out who she is yet. I couldn't even find information about her. Granted, my investigative resources are a little tight right now." Vanessa gestured to the busyness of the squad room.

Reilly focused on Vanessa's words. She was talking about Carey. Reilly cleared his throat. "I get the sense she lives a pretty solitary life." Was forced to live a solitary life.

Vanessa lifted her brow. "But no one has come forward claiming to know her. That almost never happens."

Reilly shrugged. "The picture wasn't crystal clear. And she's new to the area."

Vanessa blew out her breath. "We ran the prints from the pepper spray and came up with nothing. You've been spending time with her. Any reason to believe once we figure out who she is, it'll wreck the case?"

Reilly shook his head. If anything, spending time with Carey had shown her to be strong, capable and intelligent. He could have guessed running her prints would come back empty. She wasn't a criminal. "No drugs. No alcohol. No behavior that sends up red flags." Plenty of yellow flags, though, in her secretiveness. But whatever and whoever she was running from— he guessed it wouldn't discredit her or hurt their case.

"Keep me in the loop. Let me know if you find anything," Vanessa said. "I want to know before the media does."

Reilly stood. "I will. You do the same."

Leaving the lieutenant's office and entering the pandemonium, he stopped to talk to a few buddies, ignoring the newspapers on their desks with Carey's picture, and then left the police station. He wanted the media waiting outside to snap his picture and they willingly obliged him.

"Detective, is it true that the witness for the case is in rehab?" one of the reporters shouted at him.

He ignored the question. He wasn't permitted to respond. But they didn't give up. They wanted Carey's identity and information.

"Is it true the police believe the killer is a member of a satanic cult?" another asked.

"Is the witness enrolled in the witness protection program?"

Ludicrous. Every last question. But it didn't stop the worry from mounting. When Reilly brought Carey in for a lineup, he'd be on high alert.

He was tired from the long drive, tired of listening to questions slandering Carey. He went to a nearby diner to refuel, taking a seat at the counter and ordering a turkey club. The diner was busy at this hour and Reilly ate slowly. The more people who saw him without Carey the better.

Carey. Maybe it was better for her not to be seen with him, but he preferred when she was close. His family would take care of her, but it would make him feel better when he was back at the ranch where he could see her, talk to her, touch her.

He'd crossed the line with her several times and instead of sating his need, it had increased it exponentially. It was harder and harder to see her only as the witness in this case, a woman who needed his help. The passion in her kiss lingered in his mind. When she'd been in his lap, he'd seen a side of her that made his blood run hot.

Blocking those thoughts, Reilly finished his meal and paid, leaving a generous tip. After a few more stops, eyes and ears open, Reilly could return to the ranch. He could have stayed overnight at his place, but he was eager to see Carey. His family would have called if anything had happened, but he was on edge.

And, despite his best efforts to feel nothing and build boundaries, he'd missed her.

By the time he was ready to leave Denver, Reilly had overheard more conversations about the Vagabond Killer, the reward being offered and the witness in the last few hours than he had in the last few weeks.

Not wanting to listen to more about the case, Reilly decided against tuning in to a news station on his eight-hour drive to Montana. Instead he found a local station playing holiday songs. It was easy to hum along with the familiar melodies. And though he tried to avoid it, the songs about family and having someone at Christmas flipped Carey into his mind. She was an easy thought to settle on.

When he thought of his family, he saw her with them. When he thought of cuddling by the fire, she was in his arms. It might not be appropriate, but eight hours alone on the road gave him too much time to think.

Denying, avoiding and suppressing his feelings for Carey wasn't working. He needed to tell her how he felt, at least, let her know that after this case was over, he wanted to see her again. Spend time with her. Get to know her.

The highway was quiet this time of night. He took a southern route out of the city, checking his rearview mirror for signs he was being followed. Taking note of a few cars behind him, he kept his pace steady. Most cars changed lanes and zipped ahead of him and some turned off the highway. One car remained on his tail, a dark blue sedan with tinted windows.

Reilly changed lanes, moving to the far right and decreasing his speed. The sedan did the same.

Irritation mixed with adrenaline. Should he attempt to pull the car over and confront the driver? If it was the man chasing Carey, he had more than a few words to say to him.

The time of night and the risk had him thinking twice. He'd have to lose the sedan. If the driver believed Reilly would lead him to Carey, hopefully his misleading direction out of the city would have the man confused about Carey's whereabouts.

Reilly didn't let on he was aware he was being followed. He drove for two miles until he saw signs for a shopping district. He took the exit and proceeded toward the center of the shopping area. The sedan followed. Reilly would lose him in the chaos and traffic of last-minute Christmas shoppers.

Reilly caught a lucky break when a mass transit bus pulled between him and the sedan. He snickered at the honking horn of the frustrated sedan driver. Out of his line of sight, Reilly sped through a yellow light and made a right turn off the main road onto a side street. It took him thirty minutes to weave his way in the correct direction toward Montana.

It was time well spent. This time, he wasn't followed.

Keeping his eyes and ears open, Reilly stopped once for gas and food, and neared Ashland around 11:00 p.m. He called his father to alert him he was almost home—he didn't want the same kind of welcome Carey had given Brady.

An hour later Reilly pulled into the driveway, hungry, tired and aching to see Carey. He told himself for the hundredth time he couldn't touch her—not now, not until this was over. He'd find a way to stop himself. He was disciplined. He could control himself. He'd talk with her and explain about Lucas, his former partner, and the mistakes he'd made. Mistakes he didn't want repeated.

Reilly opened the front door and knocked the snow off his boots on the mat. Disabling the alarm, he closed the door and set it again. When he turned, Carey was in the hallway, staring at him with wide eyes. The sight of her socked him in the gut with lust. He forgot how to breathe, his every sense trained on her.

The red hair was gone, a dark mahogany color in its place. She wore a long robe, her calves bare, and he wondered what she had on beneath it. Less than a minute into the house and he was ready to strip her clothes off and make love to her in the hallway. So much for control and discipline, reasoning and rationalizations. Every word he'd planned to say to her flew out of his mind.

As different as she looked, he was forced to see a new side of her. Carey, the woman, not Carey, the runaway and witness. And when he didn't have that visual reminder that she was a woman in trouble, his thoughts wandered into dangerous territory.

"Hey, you," Carey said. "I waited up." Her hands were jammed into the pockets of the robe. Was she cold? He'd love to warm her against his body.

He struggled to control the reaction of his lower half and his thoughts. Stick to the case. The facts. Ignore how she looked. "I don't have much to tell you about the case. Vanessa's working on a few things and she thinks they'll catch the killer soon."

She stepped closer. "I'm glad you're home safe. I was worried."

He'd been worried about her, too, but admitting it would close the distance and he needed every inch in place to keep from touching her. "The media is making a circus of the Vagabond Killer trial. They've got the picture of you at the police station and the sketch of the killer splashed everywhere."

Carey went rigid and the corners of her mouth turned down. She took another step closer. She was near enough he could reach out and touch her. He wanted to take her in his arms and tell her everything would be all right. He would make this work out for her.

"Are you trying to make me change my mind about staying involved in the case?" she asked.

Reilly blew out his breath. He didn't know what he was doing. She was making it hard to think. "No. Yes. Maybe. Until I was there for myself, I didn't realize how insane it had gotten."

Carey squared her shoulders. "I've already made up my mind. I'm going to do this. Your mom prepped me today. I look different and I feel different. I can do this."

Reilly's eyes swept over her face and across her hair. The dark color softened her. It was shorter. And looked great. His defenses were lying in shambles. "You look different."

"Your mom helped me. Brady and Harris liked it."

Of course they did. She looked beautiful. "I never said I didn't."

"I thought about you today." Her tone left no question to the manner in which she was referring.

They could not tread here. What was it he had planned to say? Why was it so hot in here? "Carey, I—"

She pressed her finger across his lips. "Don't. Please

don't feed me that line about how I'm the witness and you're the detective. We've crossed the line a dozen times and I've crossed it twenty times that often in my imagination."

He was barely holding on to his self-control. Lust enveloped him and he ached to reach out and touch her. "We can't. This isn't the time."

Carey shook her head. "You're wrong. Now is the only time we have."

His visions of their future burst in his head. She only wanted something for now. Or maybe the present was all she had to give.

But *now* was tempting. *Now* was nearly irresistible.

Getting involved with her could blow the case. Result in catastrophe. Destroy his reputation. He could only think to take her outside, where the cold would dull his raging libido. Where he wouldn't be so tempted.

Reilly looked tired, dark circles rimming his eyes. A day's worth of facial hair covered his jaw. He took off his gloves, scrubbed a hand across his face and gave her a long, penetrating look. "Get dressed."

"What?" Carey shook her head. Get dressed? "Why? Are we going somewhere?"

"Get dressed and meet me at the back door in five minutes. I want to show you something."

Unsure where he wanted to go and why, Carey scrambled upstairs to pull on her jeans and a warm sweater. Her mind was a fog of questions, but she blotted them out. She'd learned to take the moments when she was given them.

She grabbed her borrowed boots and crept downstairs. Reilly was waiting in the kitchen, holding a jacket and scarf for her. He helped her into the jacket and wrapped the scarf around her neck, lifting her hair over it.

Reilly zipped his jacket. In a hushed tone, he nodded toward the pockets. "Gloves inside."

She pulled free the thick gloves and slid them onto her fingers. He disabled the alarm and opened the door, taking her hand in his. "Watch your step. It's icy."

It was eerily quiet outside, the full moon and the soft glow of the security lights surrounding the Truman house providing light for her to see ahead of them.

"Where are we going?" she asked.

"You'll see."

They walked in the opposite direction of the barn, threading their way through a copse of pine trees. She was breathing heavily, the cold air biting into her lungs, her eyes adjusting to the dark. The quiet was pervasive, except for the sound of boots crunching through snow.

The pine trees ended abruptly, giving way to a sloped snow-covered field, rocks peaking beneath the mounds of white.

"This is beautiful," Carey said as they walked across the field, their footprints marring the perfectly crisp blanket of snow.

"Close your eyes," Reilly said, taking her elbows in his hands.

She did as he asked and he guided her another twenty steps. She slipped once, but Reilly's hand came to her waist, steadying her. Her body temperature elevated and razor sharp desire pierced her.

He stopped and turned her ninety degrees to the left. He stood behind her, his breath hot on her ear. "Open them."

She opened her eyes and sucked in her breath. The land dropped off sharply three feet in front of them.

From this location on the mountain, she could see into the deep valley below, covered in green trees trimmed in white. Mountain ridges rose up on the other side, spearing into the clouds above.

"Brady and I found this place when we were younger."

Carey peered over her shoulder at him. He wasn't looking at the magnificence spread for miles in every direction. He was looking at her, his eyes burning with heat, his cheeks flushed with cold. Maybe his resistance was only marginally better than hers. She held his gaze for a long, loaded moment. "Thank you for sharing this with me."

He looped his arms around her waist and she turned her body to his, lifting her face. She felt herself drowning in him, wishing bulky coats didn't separate them and they could be skin to skin, wrapped in each other's arms.

"I shouldn't do this. I've been thinking about it all day, but I shouldn't. You're so beautiful and I can't stop wanting you." His mouth settled on hers, his lips cool, his tongue hot as it invaded her mouth. He angled his head to kiss her deeply, to let his tongue parry with hers. The kiss was thoroughly arousing. His hands spread across her back, holding her against him, possessive, safe. Jean-clad thighs brushed, electricity igniting between them. Emotions she had tried to suppress roared to life. Rocking his hips into hers, the friction of denim against her body sent a tremor of excitement through her.

"Tell me your real name," he said, moving his mouth to her cheek. "Let me say your name. Let me have that part of you."

She let her head fall back as he loosened the scarf

from around her neck and tickled a path along the column of her throat with his lips. The cold night air didn't bother her with Reilly's heat melting it away. "You already have me." Had already had her. Maybe since the moment they'd met, on some level, that connection had always stretched between them.

His lips brushed left to right across the sensitive skin of her neck. "Please. Your real name. You can tell me. I'm not going to hurt you."

She squeezed her eyes shut as warnings assaulted her, warring with her heart to keep her secret. She tried to think of some way around this, something she could say that wouldn't make him pull away. He wasn't playing fair, wasn't giving her a chance as he continued his pleasurable torment, returning his lips to hers and tightening his hands in her hair.

His mouth was insistent. She could feel the tension heighten in her body. He didn't pose the question to her again. He didn't have to. Maybe she was a fool for trusting him, for believing he would be different than the other people in her life who had let her down. But in this moment she tossed care to the wind. She took a leap of faith, praying she wouldn't live to regret it.

She set her hands on the side of his face and tore her mouth away. "My name is Haley."

"Haley," he repeated. He let a note of wonder into his voice.

She waited for his reaction, to see if he would mentally tick through the possibilities of who she could be, but the gentle stroke of his hands took away her worry. "Haley," he said again. Her name on his tongue shook her to her soul. It had been too long since someone had spoken her name with that level of warmth, that level of reverence.

He returned his mouth to hers and kissed her until the world faded away and it was she and Reilly, panting and breathless, passion searing her to the core.

Reilly held her to him, nipping at her ears with his mouth. "You're cold. Let's go home."

She didn't protest, though she wasn't cold. Wrapped in the warm circle of his embrace, the cold and the snow couldn't diffuse the heat spreading across her chest.

They hiked back to the house, Reilly's hands never leaving her body. Arousal thrummed in her blood. His kiss burned on her lips. Inside the house, after shedding their snow gear, they again stood at the door to her bedroom. This time Reilly followed her inside. Her heartbeat quickened when he closed the distance between them.

Her skin prickled with simmering awareness and she ached for his touch. His eyes never left her. She unsnapped and unzipped her jeans and wiggled out of them. He knelt on the floor in front of her and pulled them lower, touching her sides lightly.

"How are your bruises?" he asked, concern edging his voice. His hands stroked her skin, evoking an immediate reaction.

"They're better. They only hurt sometimes," she said, though she hadn't completely registered the question. He stood slowly and lifted her sweater over her head.

He reached for the clasp of her bra and waited for her to respond, to give him the green light. She nodded slowly. With practiced fingers he opened the clasp and she let her arms down, sending the bra to the floor.

His eyes lingered on hers for a moment before sweeping down her body. He set his hands on her hips and brought her close to him and kissed her, a scorching kiss, his lips playing with hers. He brought his hands to her breasts, cupping them in his palms. She let out a small moan, a sound he captured with his mouth.

His hands tweaked the hardened peaks of her nipples. "Are you cold?"

"No," she said, forking her fingers into his hair. She was hot. Ready. Wanting.

He lowered his mouth to her breasts and suckled one at a time as she held his face in her hands.

Walking her toward the bed, he lowered her and moved his body over hers.

"You're still wearing clothes," she protested.

"I know." His mouth moved to her stomach, kissed a path around her navel.

She grasped the hem of his shirt and tugged at it, wanting to feel his bare skin against hers. She didn't want anything between them. He lifted his arms and tossed the shirt away, lowering himself on top of her. His hot skin brushed against her and she closed her arms around him.

He reached between her thighs, parting them, running his fingers across her oversensitive skin. He growled low in his throat. When he spoke her name, Haley, it tingled in her ears. She closed her eyes and took a slow deep breath, inhaling the scent of him, letting the heat of his body pour over her.

The longer his body was pressed to hers, the hotter she felt, the hungrier she was to have him. She arched her hips against his hand in invitation, opening her legs wider and pulling him between them.

He moved over her, teasing, drawing out the anticipation until his name escaped her lips in a frantic demand.

There was the crinkling of foil and then his body left hers for a moment. When he maneuvered on top of her again, she splayed her legs. His hands went beneath her, lifting her and tilting her hips. Yes, this was what she wanted. An eternity of anticipation raced through her.

Then, finally, he sank into her. She nearly vaulted off the bed from the sensations exploding from her core throughout her body. They fit perfectly.

He stilled for a long moment before withdrawing almost completely. She grasped his hips, pulling him hard and deep inside her, setting the pace she liked, showing him what she loved.

Pleasure rippled through her with every thrust. The connection to another, the intimacy blossoming between them, the exquisite tenderness of the moment making her feel more alive than she had in years.

She held nothing back, taking him deep, melting into the moment. His mouth found hers, capturing her lips in a kiss that moved in harmony with the rest of his body.

She lost herself, tumbled and fell, her body finding the ultimate release. Moments later he crashed with her in a tangle of arms and legs, breathless pants, and ripples of pleasure.

As their breathing returned to normal, Reilly eased away from her.

He kissed her cheek. "Give me a minute."

When he returned, he slid beneath the sheets. With a sigh of contentment, Carey gave him her back and nestled her hips against his hard, hot body. He slung his arm around her waist and held her close. His breath tickled her neck and his heart beat against her back.

She closed her eyes and gave in to sleep, feeling warm and protected in Reilly's arms.

Taking Carey to one of the most beautiful spots in the county and then making love to her hadn't been his best-laid plan.

And the further he sank into his attraction for her, the less he thought about the consequences. He needed to put his job first and his personal feelings second. She believed they had only *now*. Wasn't he a better cop than that? He'd find a way to give them a *later*.

As soon as they touched, they both went up in flames. Surrender was inevitable, his defenses in shambles.

Reilly awoke when the sun peeked over the horizon line. Cuddled against him was a sleeping Carey, her brown hair half-covering her face and her body tucked into his. She was warm, her skin was soft, and it was hell extracting himself from her bed. He climbed over her and tiptoed to his room, getting into the bottom bunk, careful to avoid Harris's leg that had fallen over the side of the bed.

He couldn't allow her to wake next to him. Those intimacies would give her the wrong impression. He'd planned to come here and talk to her. Get her to agree erecting some fences between them was a good idea. Instead he'd seen her and lost the ability to construct a logical argument as to why building fences was a good idea.

"Did you at least tell her you were leaving?" Harris asked.

Reilly should have known better than to think Harris wouldn't have noticed him slipping into the room. "No. She'll understand."

"Or you'll hurt her more than she already is."

"Don't try that psychobabble on me."

"It's not psychobabble. It's women. They don't like it when you lie, hide things or do something without an explanation."

"I can handle this," Reilly said, though he wasn't sure he could.

Harris shifted on the bed above him, causing the springs to squeak. "I like her. We all like her. Mom will be pissed if you hurt her."

It was the last thing he wanted, as well. But she had to understand it was his job to protect her. They needed some boundaries. "I'm not going to hurt her. I'm doing everything I can to see she isn't hurt."

Harris scoffed. "Physically, sure. Any one of us would take a bullet for her. But what about how she feels? Who's taking care of that?"

Sometimes he hated that his family was this close and that his brother loved to dig into his family's psyches. Reilly preferred when they didn't talk about feelings, but in that regard, his training was turning Harris into the sister he'd never had. "I've never felt like I had a sister before this morning," Reilly said, trying to deflect some of the guilt he felt by ragging on Harris.

"I'm trying to help you out. I see how you look at her and how she looks at you. At the very least give her the respect she deserves."

Reilly wasn't trying to be a weasel who didn't bother saying goodbye. He needed to have some boundaries to avoid a fallout that would destroy the Vagabond Killer's court case or force an awkward situation neither of them could diffuse and, therefore, one of them would have to leave. Carey would have to move out and get protection from another member of the squad and no one would be more careful with her than he would. No one else would see to it she had everything she needed.

If only he knew more about the man Carey was running from. Keeping her away from the media was one thing. Keeping her out of the hands of an abusive ex-boyfriend was another.

"I'll talk to her," Reilly said and closed his eyes,

trying to catch a little more sleep. His mind wouldn't settle and an hour passed before he drifted into a light slumber.

He woke when he heard Carey moving around in his room. Reilly got out of bed and instead of entering through the bathroom door as he had in the past, he knocked on the door to the hallway. Carey opened it a quarter of the way.

"Morning," he said.

The corner of her mouth lifted. "That was going to be my line."

"How'd you sleep?"

A long moment passed, thick and palpable. They spoke at the same time. "When did you leave?" she asked.

"Last night shouldn't have happened," he said.

She retreated a step and hurt flickered across her face. "I see. Well then. I need to take a shower. I'll see you at breakfast."

With that, she closed the door in his face.

Harris chose that moment to walk by and clap Reilly on the shoulder. "Nice job. Maybe next time you could get it done faster and shoot her."

Chapter 8

Reilly's cell phone vibrated on his hip. Lifting it from the cradle, he watched Carey and his mom in the kitchen making bread. Carey hadn't spoken to him since that morning and it had become a silent punishment—watching her in all her graceful beauty and not talking to her or touching her. Though he'd caused the lingering awkwardness, he didn't know how to fix it.

He glanced at the phone. Vanessa's name lit on the display and he answered.

"We got him. Last night. Coming out of a convenience store."

Adrenaline surged in his veins. "How cliché."

Vanessa chuckled. "You're telling me. You need to get the witness back here pronto. He has a lawyer and if he's sprung, he'll be gone. We won't get a second chance at him."

"I know you, Van. You'll find a way to hold him until we get there."

"I'm not taking chances with this. The other victim is awake, but he doesn't remember anything about the attack. Get the witness here. Now."

They had the Vagabond Killer in custody. But the guy Carey was running from was still out there. "We're going to need cover. I don't want the media crawling all over our witness." At the word *witness,* Carey looked up from the bowl she was mixing.

"She needs to do the lineup and I might not be able to keep the hounds off her back completely."

Reilly stifled an argument. Vanessa knew what she was doing and his concerns for Carey shouldn't supersede ensuring the Vagabond Killer stayed behind bars. How much of this case fell on Carey's shoulders? The Vagabond Killer had left DNA evidence at one of the crime scenes, but Vanessa had the burden of proof. She wouldn't want to risk the killer's lawyer drumming up reasons for how his client's DNA ended up at the scene, throwing reasonable doubt over the case. They needed a positive ID. "I'll get her safely to the lineup if you make sure the lineup stays out of the media."

He couldn't have a repeat of the past, couldn't allow a killer to go free. The Vagabond Killer had to stay behind bars where he belonged. Lives were at stake if he was released on bail.

He and Carey were taking a chance going into the city, possibly getting caught in the media storm. Reporters and photographers would be looking for her. It was a careful balancing act. He wanted justice for the Vagabond Killer's victims, but he also wanted justice for Carey.

"Reilly, you there?" Vanessa asked.

Realizing he'd been staring at Carey, he looked away. "Yeah, sorry about that."

"Don't get distracted. Tell you what. Plan to be somewhere near Denver, but we'll keep the specifics as last-minute as possible. I'll go for the middle of the night, 2:00 a.m., for the lineup and text you the location."

"You think you can get the suspect's lawyer to agree to that?" Reilly asked.

Vanessa snorted. "I've got the mayor and the D.A. desperate to put this guy away. They'll make sure I get what I need to wrap this up before Christmas."

If Vanessa said she could pull it off, Reilly wasn't complaining. "Not a problem. I'll take care of things on my end." Reilly snapped closed his phone and turned to the anxious eyes of his mother and Carey. His mother waited for him to speak. Carey drummed her fingers on the counter.

"They caught the Vagabond Killer. They need you in the city for a lineup," Reilly said. He hated speaking the words, hated knowing they'd scare her.

Carey went still. "I guess there's no way around this." At least she was speaking to him again.

"I'm sorry, Carey. We need you. A sketch isn't as reliable in court as an ID."

Her shoulders stiffened. "Court? Who said anything about going to court?"

Reilly winced. So much for tact. "You'll need to testify at some point." She knew this. She might have been denying it, hoping something would change, but she knew it.

She shook her head and went to the sink. "No. The lineup is it. I can't stay through a trial. He'll find me. He'll kill me."

Guilt hammered him. This was difficult for her.

"We'll do everything in our power to ensure you're safe."

Carey glared at him, her blue eyes impassioned. "Even that might not be enough."

A slap at his pride. "Have we done something to make you feel unsafe?"

Carey washed her hands and dried them roughly with a paper towel. "You can't watch me around the clock in Denver like you can here. You can't follow me around and stay while I'm at work. And no way would I expect that. You have a life of your own. But without you, I don't feel safe."

The impact of her words hit him low and hard. She had trusted him and he had shaken that trust with his behavior earlier that morning. "It can be the same as it is now. We'll find a safe place to live and I'll watch over you."

Carey braced her hands on the counter. "For how long? A trial could drag on for months, maybe years. You don't know who this Vagabond Killer is or how much money he has. He could appeal and add months to the process. In that time, do you really believe you'll keep the media away from the courthouse? Do you think Mark won't find me? He's already looking for me."

She sucked in her breath, obviously realizing she'd said too much. Jane set her hand on Carey's back, rubbing it consolingly. Reilly wanted to console her, too, but he also wanted blood. Mark. The man who had terrorized her was named Mark. Fury sizzled in his veins. There had to be thousands of Marks in America, but it was a start. Reilly would find him. Mark would not hurt Carey.

"He won't find you. We'll keep you hidden."

Carey threw up her hands. "How? I've tried to hide. I

changed my hair, my clothes, my city, my job, my name. I don't talk to people in my old life. I don't use credit cards or keep any of the same habits. He's a criminal with powerful connections. He'll find me."

Jane touched Carey's hair. "You look much different with your hair dark. Most people will have remembered the red from the picture. I've gotten in and out of places by dressing and acting a certain way. I saw that picture of you on the news. You're a new woman now."

Yes, she was. Last night he'd seen a new side of Carey. Sensual Carey. Amazingly tempting. His body tightened as the memories replayed in his mind.

Carey's eyes connected with his. Was she remembering last night, too? "You don't have to do this for me. You don't owe me anything."

He never *had* to do anything. He wanted to keep her safe. It was as natural an instinct as breathing. "It's my job to keep you safe and I take it to heart."

She leveled him a look. "When this is over, if I live to testify against the Vagabond Killer, I'll still be in danger."

Reilly refused to accept that as true. Every instinct told him he could bring this to a close. He could protect her and hunt down Mark. "Let me protect you. Let me do my job and find Mark. You can sleep at night knowing he'll never hurt you again. Never."

Jane looked between Reilly and Carey, her lips pressed into a thin line of worry.

Carey stared at the floor. "You don't know him. He's not like regular men. He's not even like the Vagabond Killer. He doesn't do his own dirty work. He pays someone to do it for him. And he pays well because he wants the best. I don't stand a chance against the men that work for Mark. And what about you and your family? What if he tries to hurt you?" Worry flooded her face.

Reilly could handle this. Her concern was unneeded, though it did please him that she cared. "He's not going to do anything to you or anyone else because when I see him, he's done."

Carey dragged a hand through her hair, shoving it behind her ears. "You don't know how powerful he is. You don't know the kinds of things he's capable of."

Reilly set his jaw. "You're right. But I've never run from someone who needed my help. You need my help."

Carey took a deep breath and let it out. She closed her eyes for a few moments and then opened them. "Let's get through this lineup. After that, I'll see what I can do."

Quiet rage at the man who had hurt her hummed inside him. How sick was Mark that Carey was more afraid of him than a serial killer?

Reilly could sense Carey's tension. The long drive to Denver didn't give her much else to do except think. Think about Mark. Think about the Vagabond Killer case. And unless his instincts were off, think about him and what had happened between them.

He wanted to be honest with her. It might clear the air and make her feel better. "I need to tell you something that I should have told you before." Before he had slept with her. Before he had let himself get involved that deeply with her.

She seemed surprised that he'd broken the silence that had stretched between them since they'd left his parents' house. "Sounds ominous, but go ahead."

It was more difficult to find the words than he'd imagined. "When I was a rookie detective, my partner Lucas made the mistake of getting too close to a victim on a case. He felt bad for her and wanted to make things better."

Carey didn't say anything, just watched him from the passenger seat with deep, soulful eyes.

"When it was time for her to testify, the defense twisted Lucas's relationship into something inappropriate." Thinking of it made him angry all over again. "They accused him of coaching her with details of the crime and by the time they were done, the jury didn't believe her testimony. The defendant walked. Not guilty on all counts."

Carey's eyes softened with compassion and she reached out and squeezed his upper arm. "Reilly, I'm sorry. That's awful."

"Lucas had to resign, and for months the department was under scrutiny by the public and by lawyers. It was a disaster. The worst part was, the guy struck again two weeks later. That time, he made sure the victim didn't live to testify against him."

A death for which Reilly felt responsible. If he had seen what Lucas was doing, if he had talked to Lucas before it went too far, there wouldn't have been a second victim. The criminal would have spent the rest of his days in prison. "I blame myself for not seeing it."

"You can't blame yourself for someone else's actions. I'm sure you did everything you could."

He could have done more. "I never want that situation to play itself out again. I don't want the Vagabond Killer or Mark to walk free because of how I feel for you. I want you to have the life you deserve and that means not living in fear."

Her thumb stroked his arm. "My identification and

testimony for either case has nothing to do with you. Anything I saw happened before I met you."

He wanted to see the difference. How he felt for Carey was unlike his feelings for any other woman. The intensity alone was soul-shaking. "I want to believe that. I want a *jury* to believe that. I want Mark and the Vagabond Killer caught and put away so you're safe. That's why we can't be involved now."

Her eyes darkened with sadness. "That's why you said we shouldn't have slept together."

At his nod of affirmation, Carey continued. "Even if they catch the Vagabond Killer, charging Mark could take years. And he'll weasel out of whatever cage you try to put him in. Even in prison, he would find a way to have someone come for me."

No. Reilly wouldn't allow that. This time the case was going to play itself out on his terms. They'd catch the Vagabond Killer and Mark and, with Carey's help, send them to prison for the rest of their miserable lives.

"He's not going to find you. I'm going to find him and then I'm going to take him down."

Carey let his words replay through her mind. Reilly was trying to explain his behavior, which she had found herself at odds with sometimes. His behavior the night before had hurt her. "Have you considered the possibility that if Mark goes down, he'll take me with him?"

That seemed to startle Reilly. His tone took on a seriousness she'd never heard from him before. "If there is something you've done that could come out when we find him, you need to tell me now."

When she thought back over her life, she could pinpoint a hundred things she'd seen or heard that she'd ignored and shouldn't have. She would have to tread carefully here, not wanting to bring more trouble her way. "I can list a hundred events that are subject to scrutiny. I was dating a very bad man. Some people would find me guilty by association."

"I can best protect you if I know everything."

Carey closed her eyes and inhaled deeply. This was ground over which she hadn't wanted to tread. "Anything I know is speculation. I can't prove anything."

"Then what are you afraid of?" His voice was soft and tender.

"Mark could twist the activities of a saint. He could say I knew what he was doing and that I did nothing."

"Did you?"

She shook her head, closing her eyes to hold the tears that threatened to spill out and slip down her cheeks. "Not until the end." Not until her father had died did she question his life. Her life. Their life.

"Then you don't have a reason to be afraid."

Reilly only wanted to see the best-case scenario, ending with Mark and the Vagabond Killer being caught and her walking away unscathed. "You don't know Mark. He'll pick up on the guilt I feel. How did I not know?" She opened her eyes and tears ran down her cheeks. "I should have guessed. I should have asked questions or paid attention. I was old enough to know something was wrong."

He reached over and squeezed her hand. "It's not a crime to know something. You were scared. You did your best. No court will hold you responsible for staying quiet."

In an ideal world that was true. Her world was corrupt and dirty. "Depends which court. Mark has bribed plenty of law enforcement officers, judges and clerks. What would stop him from buying favorable rulings?"

"He can't buy me."

Carey considered that. No, Reilly wouldn't be bought. He'd resisted the temptation and he wouldn't sell her out for money. But what if he found out who she was? Would his feelings for her change? Would he stop wanting to protect her?

What about the risk to his family? If their lives were in danger, would Reilly back down? She wouldn't expect him to put their safety before her. "You have other liabilities."

He caught her meaning quickly. "If someone went after my family, they are more than capable of taking care of themselves. My dad is pretty laid-back, but if anyone tried to hurt my mom, he'd take them out. No questions asked."

Carey felt a pang somewhere in her heart. Had her father felt that way about her? He had shielded her from his business and kept her on a tight leash. But where had she ranked in his life? "You're lucky to have people in your life who care about you that much."

"You have someone in your life who cares about you."

Reilly's actions had shown it, but she wanted the words. She inclined her head.

He laid his hand over hers. "Me."

One word that delivered volumes. Reilly cared for her. He trusted her. And the crazy thing was, she felt the same about him. Could she have a future with Reilly? Had he been right all along, that Mark and the Vagabond Killer could be caught and jailed, leaving her free to live her life?

In many ways, she couldn't fixate on those hopes. Reilly didn't know who she was. If he did, everything would change.

It wouldn't take him long to piece together who she was. Haley and Mark were common enough names, but a detective would figure it out. Father who'd died recently. Woman on the run. Reilly would learn about her past and then he'd change his mind about helping her. Why would he want to help the daughter of a criminal?

"Do you really think this is going to work?" she asked.

"What is 'this'?"

Every question seemed to take on two meanings: their forbidden relationship and the problem with the Vagabond Killer and Mark. She wasn't pressing him about their relationship. He'd been clear about his reasons for not wanting to be involved with her. "Getting into the city without someone seeing me."

"We've come up with a pretty solid plan. No one knows the exact location of the lineup except my boss and Vanessa. We'll take care of the lineup, Vanessa's arranged a safe place for us to stay the night and we'll be back at the ranch by tomorrow afternoon."

Information had a way of leaking. A reporter could be in the right place at the right time and recognize her. "Do you think Mark will be waiting for me in the city?"

A muscle in Reilly's jaw ticked. "He might be in the city, but he won't know where the lineup is. We've asked the Vagabond Killer's lawyer to use discretion to protect your privacy."

The nagging feeling wouldn't let go of her thoughts. "But if he is?"

"If he is, I'll be ready for him." He reached for her hand and squeezed it, letting go after a few seconds. She read comfort and support in his gesture, felt the flare of desire and smothered it. White Knight syndrome again. It ran rampant in the Truman family. Reilly had no idea what he was saying or who he was going up against.

He must have sensed her apprehension. "You'll be at my side whenever we're in public places and if he shoots at me, he'll be shooting at an officer. An armed officer," Reilly added.

She hated guns, but knowing Reilly had protection soothed her nerves. Mark was vicious and he'd hurt anyone who got in his way. His words from the news clip sprung into her mind. *We have one legal issue we're close to eliminating.* A chill shuddered inside her. If she didn't warn Reilly about Mark and who he was and what he could do, Reilly wouldn't know how to best protect himself. Mark wasn't a petty criminal with a checkered past. He was an all-out, career criminal. Telling Reilly the truth about Mark could help, but it could also give Reilly enough clues to uncover her identity. Wouldn't he figure it out eventually? Was it best to tell him and get it over with? What if he got hurt because she didn't tell him how to prepare?

Reilly's phone buzzed and he handed it to her. "That's probably Vanessa. Can you read the text?"

Carey took the phone and opened the text. "It says 2:00 a.m., Lakewood police station."

"Great." He glanced at the clock. "We'll be on time."

Carey flipped the station on the radio, needing music to distract her from her worries. She listened listlessly to the radio and closed her eyes, pretending to be asleep, buying herself time to think about her next move and how she was going to protect Reilly.

At 1:00 a.m., Reilly received a second text message from Vanessa.

"She says 2:00 a.m., Commerce City police station," Carey said. "Why would she change the location?"

Reilly glanced at her. "Probably another part of the

plan to keep the information from leaking. She's cutting it close though. But we'll get there. Don't worry about it."

Carey wasn't worried about making the lineup on time. She was worried about getting in and out without incident.

At 2:00 a.m., they pulled into the Commerce City police station.

"I don't know this station or these officers, so stick close," Reilly said, circling the car to the rear of the building.

Close to Reilly was where she wanted to be. He parked against the sidewalk, Carey's door closest to the entrance.

Carey took a deep breath and tried to smother the chilling sense of foreboding that ignited in her gut. As they had neared the police station, Reilly had grown more alert, his shoulders tight and his eyes seemed to take in everything around them. He was concerned, too. Or at least, he wasn't wholly unaffected by the situation.

Dark shadows concealed the farthest corners of the parking lot and several police cruisers were parked along the fence at the end of the lot. The lot was monitored with cameras.

She could do this. She remembered what the Vagabond Killer looked like and she could pick him out of a lineup. Forgetting his face was impossible. It would be over in ten minutes. She could do this for Reilly, for herself, for the city and rely on Reilly's unwavering strength to power through. Once she'd done her part, she wouldn't be obligated to stay with the Trumans. Vanessa would find a way to build her case and keep the Vagabond Killer behind bars. The thoughts should have brought her relief, but only sadness torqued through her.

"Stay in the car. Let me come around to get you," Reilly said.

Reilly got out of the car and circled the front, opening her door.

She was safe. She was with Reilly. Everything was going to be fine. She stood, staying close to his body. The memory of being in his arms simmered inside her, mixing with the warmth of nostalgia. If this was the end of the road for them, she would remember every touch, every kiss fondly and without sadness for what she'd lost when it ended.

She took a step away so he could close her door. A whizzing by her head had her turning in surprise.

Reilly shoved her back into the car and drew his gun. "Get down!"

Terror and adrenaline tore through her veins. Someone was shooting at them. What should she do?

Reilly raced around the front of the car, looking into the dark. He got in the driver's seat.

"I can't see where the shots are coming from." Reilly started the engine and shifted into Drive, jamming on the gas, sending the car lurching forward.

A bullet slammed into the rear driver's-side window. Carey yelped. "We need to call for help."

Reilly gunned the engine and sped out of the parking lot.

Carey's heart pounded so hard she couldn't hear over the sound.

"Carey," Reilly said, his voice cutting through her terror. He handed her his phone. "Dial 9-1-1. Put the phone on speaker."

With trembling fingers Carey pressed the buttons and did as Reilly asked.

"9-1-1, state your emergency." The voice was calm and professional.

"This is Detective Reilly Truman of the DPD, badge ID Adam David five seven four three. Officer requesting assistance. Shots fired in the parking lot of the Commerce City police station. I've fled the scene with a civilian."

Carey heard the dispatcher typing at her keyboard. "Are you somewhere safe?"

Reilly ignored her question. "Possible multiple shooters at large. Proceed with extreme caution."

Bile rose in her throat. Mark had found a way to get to her. How had he known she would be there?

"Do not return to the scene. Are you in a safe place, Detective Truman?" the dispatcher asked again.

"We're fine." With that Reilly disconnected the call. "Call Vanessa," Reilly said and swore. "We're being followed." He jammed the gas and the engine roared louder. "Carey, slouch down low."

Carey did as he asked. She found Vanessa's number in his address book and called. The phone rang four times, then Vanessa answered. Carey put the call on speakerphone.

"Where are you? When you didn't show, I thought you were dead," Vanessa said. The worry was evident in the shrillness of her voice.

The car shuddered as Reilly hit the brakes and whipped the car onto the on-ramp to the highway. "We just left the Commerce City police station."

"What were you doing there? I texted you to come to the Lakewood police station."

Reilly and Carey exchanged glances. "I got two text messages from you. The first said Lakewood and the second said Commerce City."

"I only sent the one message," Vanessa said.

Dread coiled in Carey's stomach. Mark. He'd found a way to send another message from Vanessa. He could have hired computer hackers to install spyware on Vanessa's phone. Or Reilly's. Or everyone's at the police station. "Did you have the lineup schedule in your phone?" Carey asked.

Vanessa swore. "It was in my phone's calendar, but no names. Why? Do you think someone messed with my phone?"

It was precisely what Carey thought.

"We can't rule it out," Reilly said. "Look, Van, we've got someone tailing us. I can't talk now. I just needed to know you were okay."

"You and the witness need to get somewhere safe. We got the wrong guy and it's a disaster over here."

Reilly made a sharp turn off the highway. The speed and the curving road made Carey feel as if the car was going to flip.

"Wait, what do you mean you got the wrong guy?" Reilly asked through clenched teeth.

"At ten of two, we got a call from the Denver precinct. Another vic showed up in an alley in the same neighborhood as five of the other killings. Same method and same cause of death. The guy we have in custody couldn't have committed the crimes."

Carey shivered, the impact of Vanessa's words constricting her breathing. They had the wrong man. Both the Vagabond Killer and Mark were loose on the streets.

"Are you sure?" Reilly asked, running a red light at an empty intersection.

"Yes, I'm sure," Vanessa said, irritation clear in her tone. "The suspect's lawyer is demanding his immediate release and as soon as court opens, he'll get a judge to sign off on it."

"Van, I gotta go. I'll be in touch," Reilly said.

Reilly snatched the phone from Carey and shut it off. "I lost one of the cars, but the other is following us."

Carey rubbed her arms, dinner threatening to make a reprisal. "It's Mark who shot at us. He has the resources to pull something like this. He found out about the lineup and he sent you that text message."

Carey closed her eyes. Part of her nightmare was supposed to end tonight. The Vagabond Killer had been in custody, she was going to pick him out of the lineup and send him to a lifetime in prison. Now she was neck-deep in trouble. Mark had shot at her and Reilly, and the Vagabond Killer was still loose on the streets.

A pregnant pause filled the air with the sound of Reilly's car engine taking hairpin turns, wheels screaming. "Tell me why Mark wants you dead."

And the situation got worse. "It's better if you don't know." She didn't want to burden him with the things she knew about Mark. The car zipped by buildings and streets, making her feel dizzy and out of sorts. Between her terror and confusion, it was difficult to think clearly.

"It's better if I do. I've been shot at. I need to know who I'm dealing with. Abusers will go pretty far to get to their victims, but this guy is taking it to a new, sick level."

He was right. People were getting hurt because of her. This had to stop.

Another bullet pierced the back windshield. Reilly swore. "They better not hit our tires or we're screwed. Get on the floor and cover your head."

Panic renewed in her chest and Carey fought the scream of terror that rose in her throat. She did as Reilly said. Crouched on the floor, she watched Reilly's face and the determination in his eyes, scared for him, terrified he would get hurt. The car flew over the road, every bump jarring, every turn wild.

"I got the lead on him. Send up a prayer this works," Reilly said.

Reilly turned off his lights and swerved the car into an abandoned office complex parking lot, sliding the car behind the brown brick building. He left the engine running, watching the rearview mirror.

Carey plowed a hand through her hair. What if he was hurt because of her? He'd nearly been shot. "Where are we going to go? You can't take me to your parents' ranch. We can't risk being followed. He'll find me. He will never stop looking." Her worst fear realized, she'd been a fool to think she was safe. She'd never be safe and she'd always be a danger to the people around her.

Reilly's eyes never left the mirror. "We need to think this through and figure out our next steps."

Our next steps. Implying they were in this together.

Reilly took a deep breath. "I think we lost them." He pulled the car onto the road again, scanning the area around them, and drove at a normal speed.

Carey crawled into the passenger seat, her legs feeling weak and her arms trembling. "Tell me what you need me to do." She needed to feel useful and not like a burden.

"You can start by telling me about Mark."

Indecision weighed on her, mixing with heavy guilt. If Reilly didn't know how dangerous Mark was, he wouldn't know how to protect himself. It was a matter of time before Reilly put together the pieces, and holding back the information was going to get him killed. If he knew who she was, he might be finished protecting her. But for his safety, she had to come clean.

Knowing she was risking him being disgusted, she took a deep breath and struggled to find her voice. "Mark is a millionaire many times over. He's ruthless and he's obsessive. Right now, he's obsessed with having me dead. He knows I'm the only person in the world who can take away the life he loves."

To his credit, Reilly didn't appear fazed. "How can you do that?"

She took a deep breath. She had to force the words from her mouth and ignore the mounting trepidation that Reilly would leave her. "He's the leader of an extensive crime ring. And he knows my testimony could put him behind bars."

Chapter 9

Reilly's finger tightened around the steering wheel, his knuckles going white. "A crime boss?"

"Yes," Carey said, the word catching in her throat.

"You were involved with a criminal?"

"Yes." Once the words started, she couldn't stop them, desperation fueling the need to explain herself. "Mark Sheffield was my fiancé. He used me to get close to my father. My father owned a few restaurants on the east coast and a winery on the west coast. I can't list all the things my father did or all the people he knew. He was a powerful man."

Reilly glanced over at her, questions in his eyes. "A powerful man?"

The question spoke volumes. A powerful man in the crime world, using his legitimate businesses to launder money for wealthy friends. "Yes."

"Keep talking."

His voice didn't give away anything about what he was thinking. She imagined disgust for her growing in his gut and it made her more panicked to keep him close, to hear some words of reassurance that he'd stay.

"My father passed away. Heart trouble. And then Mark took over his businesses." She fought to control the lump forming in her throat. Dang, it hurt to talk about this. "My father had always protected me. Kept me from knowing what he did for a living." She took a deep breath. "But Mark did no such thing. I started to put things together when I was going through my father's office. When I asked Mark about it, he made it clear my father had done some bad things and he was taking over. I broke up with him the night I learned the truth."

"I'm guessing he didn't react well."

Not in the least. "He came after me. He threatened me. He stalked me. He was powerful, and my father's assets and connections helped him." Mark had made her life a living nightmare. Every time she'd turned around, he was there, sending flowers, emailing her, sending messages that were thinly veiled threats. He'd wormed his way into her father's inner circle and made her feel alone and helpless. "I was terrified of what he'd do to me." And she'd caved. She felt she had no other choice. "I told him I had shoved him away because I was afraid. We got engaged and instead of planning a wedding, I planned my escape."

"And now he wants you because you have dirt on him?"

Her best guess was that he had realized she knew far too much and wouldn't cooperate and keep quiet. "He must suspect it. And he wants complete, uncontested control of my father's assets. He was helping my father run his businesses and manage his accounts before he died and Mark took over immediately after. He was so thick into it, no one questioned him. But no judge in this country, except one he buys off, would believe whatever falsified documents Mark draws up to say my father left everything to him. If I were dead, there isn't anyone to contest it, and Mark could get a hundred people to claim he was like a son to my father. I haven't contacted Mark or gotten involved in his businesses since I ran, but I'm a loose thread he wants to tie off."

She could see Reilly working the information over in his mind. "You're the daughter of Croswell Leone?"

She started. He'd put that together fast. Then again, how many crime bosses had died in the last two years? "Feel free to eject me from the car." Her attempt at humor didn't cover how raw and exposed she felt. She waited for his response, bracing herself for his rejection. No matter what he said, she wouldn't beg him to stay. She wouldn't put him in that position. He owed her nothing. If anything, she was indebted to him.

"We're in this together. No one is ditching anyone." He glanced at her and their eyes met and held for a brief, intense moment. "Is there anything else?"

Her stomach tightened. How had he known she'd held something back? "There is one more thing." She quashed the guilt and spoke. "After I ran away from Mark, I read in the news that a good friend had been killed. Hit-and-run accident. But I don't think it was an accident. I think Mark killed her because she wouldn't tell him where I had gone." Tears burned in her eyes and Carey forced herself to finish. "But she didn't know where I'd gone. I told no one where I was. And now she's dead because of me."

Reilly's hand shot out and covered hers, and an undercurrent of heat ran between them. "No. Carey, no. You are not responsible for her death. You can't believe that. You don't know it was Mark."

But she did. In her gut, she'd known the moment she'd read the words that Mark had been behind the accident. "If I hadn't left, Tracy would still be alive."

"You've got to let go of your guilt. Mark is a monster. He hurts people. Not you."

Carey wiped at the tears streaming down her face. Speaking the words had been therapeutic, loosening some of the horror living inside her. Reilly was the first person in whom she'd confided this secret.

"I want him to pay for what he's done," Carey said, some of her guilt shifting to anger for Mark.

"He will. He won't get away with this," Reilly said.

Mark had gotten away with so much already that getting justice for Tracy wouldn't be easy.

Twenty minutes passed before Reilly spoke again. "I'm going to take care of you, Carey. You'll be safe."

Her heart surged and she wanted to crawl into his lap and bury her head in his shoulder, lose herself in the protection in his arms. She pressed her hands in her lap to keep from touching him. "I want you to be safe, too."

Reilly tossed her a look, as if to say, of course I'll be safe. "We need to find a place to stay where we can stash the car. No one is following us now, but I don't trust our luck to hold."

Reilly set a comforting hand on her leg and heat spiraled through her veins. The need for consolation and for Reilly was all-consuming. He was next to her, the physical distance less than a foot, but she felt emotionally raw and wanted another taste of the closeness she knew she'd find with him.

Reilly took another side street, maneuvering through

the city. He didn't move his hand from her thigh and that connection ignited molten-hot pleasure, leaving no part of her unaffected. "You're safe at the ranch."

She set her hand over his, gripping it, feeling as if he was the lifeline keeping her afloat. "Maybe. How long before Mark digs deep enough to find out the place belongs to your parents and comes looking for me? How do you know we won't be followed there?"

"We'll stay at a hotel tonight and get our plans in place."

She asked the question weighing on her mind. "Does it bother you who my father is? Does it bother you I was engaged to a criminal?"

His fingers flexed beneath hers. "It doesn't matter who your father was. It doesn't matter that you've made mistakes in judgment. I've been in situations where I've regretted my decisions."

Acceptance. Her heart leapt, but doubt weighed on it. "It doesn't bother you that I'm Croswell Leone's daughter?" she asked again.

"No."

He was a detective. She was the daughter of a crime boss. And he had no qualms?

"We need to get a rental car. Ours draws too much attention," Reilly said, turning onto Pena Boulevard in the direction of the airport. They ditched his car in the long-term parking lot at the airport, grabbed their bags and took a shuttle to the car rental lot. He was glad he'd thought to bring extra cash for the trip. They needed it to stay under the radar.

After talking to a sleepy attendant who didn't ask for ID and took Reilly's deposit and rental fee in cash, Reilly had the keys to a blue sedan. They got in the car and Reilly drove another thirty minutes before choosing a hotel located near a suburban town, surrounded by neighborhoods and cookie-cutter houses. "This place okay?"

Carey didn't have a preference. If he thought it was safe, she was on board. "This is fine." The longer she and Reilly were driving around, the greater the chance someone would see them or recognize her.

"I'll get a balcony room if I can. Two exits, just in case." He parked behind the building. "Pull your hood up and keep your head down. I don't want to risk anyone seeing you. Stay at my side." He wasn't making eye contact. Instead he was scanning the parking lot.

She nodded and got out of the car, jogging to match his stride into the hotel. She'd be sharing a room with Reilly. Excitement whipped through her and she calmed down by reminding herself the situation dictated the circumstances, not Reilly.

They requested a room and with the holiday, they were lucky. The hotel had a room left.

The holiday. Christmas was right around the corner and she had almost forgotten about it. Having no one to celebrate with had made holidays blend into every other day.

"Thank you for doing this," she said, laying her hand on his arm.

He tensed beneath her touch. "Just doing my job."

His words said one thing, his actions another. His actions told her he cared, he would keep her safe, and his commitment to her was as strong as it had been before he'd learned she was Croswell Leone's daughter. She wouldn't believe otherwise.

They found the elevator and took it to the second floor. They entered their room and were greeted by clean and simple décor and one king bed. Her eyes lingered on the sole mattress.

Reilly looked at her. "I can sleep on the floor."

Regardless of what he said, he didn't want to sleep on the floor. She could read it on his face. He belonged beside her. For as long as they had, they'd spend it together. His attack of conscience or his worry he was violating some unwritten rule was unnecessary. What was between them defied logic. "You slept beside me last night. Why can't you tonight?"

He said nothing for a long moment. "I don't think that's a good idea."

He was being ridiculous, but she'd respect his wishes and wouldn't press him. Her neediness might drive him further away and it was the last thing she wanted. If he preferred to draw lines between them, if he wanted to pretend they were detective and witness, then fine. She knew otherwise. And he'd see it. Even if she was long gone, he'd see it and regret not taking the moment when they had it.

Reilly needed to get away from her and *think*. Every time he looked at her, the overwhelming need to claim her sizzled in his veins. Reilly excused himself and went into the bathroom, closing the door.

His inability to squelch the burn of interest in Carey was dangerous. The last few hours had made it even more clear why he couldn't be distracted. This wasn't a vacation. He was protecting a witness from a criminal who wanted her dead.

A criminal who thought nothing of taking shots at her outside a police station. Who didn't care if he injured or killed a cop.

If Reilly didn't get his desire for her under control, he could blow the case and put her at risk.

He needed focus now more than ever. She was the daughter of Croswell Leone. One of the most ruthless and violent criminals in organized crime.

Knowing who she was strengthened the need inside him to protect her. And staying in the same hotel room with the most alluring woman he'd ever met was maddening. Sleeping together was out of the question. Would he have any resistance left with her lying next to him?

He splashed cold water on his face and returned to the bedroom.

Carey had turned down the bed and was sitting on the left side watching television. She had a faraway look in her eye as if the program hadn't kept her interest.

"What are you watching?" he asked, trying to alleviate some of the awkwardness that had bloomed between them.

"Holiday movie."

She turned her head to look at him. The muscles in his body flexed in awareness. Their eyes met and held, heat sparking between them. She felt it, too. A deep, burning need intensified.

Her eyes widened and her lips parted slightly. "I'm going to take a shower." She swallowed hard and stood, rushing into the bathroom, leaving him standing there, half-mad with lust.

A few minutes later he heard the water running. Reilly ran a frustrated hand through his hair. A thin wall separated him from a naked Carey.

He needed air. He needed to think about the case and not about her. He cracked the door on the balcony, letting a slip of fresh, cold air enter the room. He kept his attention on the bathroom in case she called for him. Is that what he wanted? For her to call out to him?

He couldn't get the image of her in the shower out of his head. If she wasn't a witness, he would have joined her in the shower and seen where it led.

The shower shut off and ten minutes later, Carey emerged from the bathroom. Her hair was combed and she'd changed into her baggy nightshirt. It hung on her curves, revealing the lines of her body.

"How was the shower?" he asked, forcing his eyes on her face, though he longed to let them wander down her body to her long, bare legs.

"Fine. The hotel soap and shampoo weren't too bad."

"I guess it's my turn then," he said. A cold shower. That would calm him. He closed the door to the balcony and locked it. "Holler if you need anything."

The shower did nothing to take his thoughts off Carey. His mind was fixated on her.

When he returned to the bedroom, Carey was curled on her side away from him, covered with the sheets and blanket. She had turned off all the lights except for the one on the far side of the bed.

"Are you cold?" he asked.

She rolled to face him. "A little. I hate hotel blankets. They're always so rough and thin."

Reilly adjusted the thermostat, turning up the temperature. "I can call the front desk and ask for another blanket."

She pulled the blanket tighter around her. "The thermostat should do it."

He didn't miss the fear and worry in her eyes. It had been a rough night for both of them. "Is there anything I can do for you? Anything you need?"

She hesitated a moment. "I'd rather not sleep alone."

He could offer her some comfort. Even if part of him knew it was a mistake, he found himself agreeing. "We can share the bed."

He walked to the side of the bed and got under the sheet and blanket. Reaching for the light on the bedside table, he turned it off. She was shivering and his resistance lasted five seconds. He reached for her and pulled her against him, tucking her into the curve of his body. She fit perfectly.

Shifting her hips, she maneuvered closer, setting her backside against his growing arousal. He looped his arm around her waist and she slid her bare foot up his calf.

"You were cold," he said against her neck, as if he needed to give her an explanation for why he'd reached for her. Her cold toes tickled the hair on his legs.

"Not anymore. I'm feeling quite toasty now."

He didn't know what to say to her, or if she expected him to say anything. She needed comfort and he was holding her to make her feel better. He closed his eyes and drifted to sleep, trying not to think about making love to her.

Reilly awoke at 6:00 a.m. with sunlight sneaking in between the dark green curtains and Carey's hot body snug against him. He'd dreamed of her, as he'd known he would. Dreamed of kissing her, of rolling on top of her, of sliding inside her. Things that shouldn't happen. Couldn't happen again. It wouldn't end well for either of them.

The cocoon of warmth beneath the blankets made getting out of bed unappealing, but if he didn't get up now, the craving building low in his gut would become unmanageable.

Trying to hold the blankets close to the mattress, Reilly slipped from the bed.

Carey moved in her sleep and her eyes opened into narrow slits. "What time is it?"

"Six. We need to get moving soon."

"Where are we going?"

As much as he hated it, they had to keep moving. He didn't like being on the defensive. Running wasn't how he handled problems, but going on the offensive with Carey in tow was dangerous. If Mark sensed he was coming after him, he had resources at his disposal to disappear.

Reilly couldn't return to his place in Denver. He had to assume Mark knew where he lived. If they moved from hotel to hotel, someone would see them or recognize Carey eventually.

The ranch was still one of his safest options. His parents had it well protected from public records. Could he return to the ranch without putting his family at risk? "I need a couple of days to gather information. Then we'll decide."

Carey scrubbed a hand over her face. "What information? I know everything about Mark. Or are you talking about the Vagabond Killer?"

"I'm talking about both." Though another killing had occurred while the Vagabond Killer was in jail, the situation made Reilly uneasy. He couldn't quite banish the niggling sensation he had overlooked something about the case.

"You want to find both?" Carey asked, sitting up in bed.

Her eyes were drowsy, her hair tousled. She looked good—too good. Reilly rolled his shoulders, trying to work out some of the pent-up tension. "Big picture—

we need to find them both. For now, I need to keep you safe. I'm going to get cleaned up. There's energy bars in the bag if you're hungry."

Carey nodded and reached for the television remote control. "I'll see if the news has something about the shooting."

Forty minutes later, Carey was sitting on the passenger seat in Reilly's car, hot coffee in one hand and a bagel from the hotel in the other. "Where are we going?"

Reilly climbed inside the car and set his takeout coffee cup in the cup holder. "To meet a friend who works in the detention center where the Vagabond Killer was being held."

"Why? He's not there anymore. I saw on the news he was released from police custody early this morning."

Reilly glanced at her. Some moments she could feel the intensity in his gaze, could sense the underlying need in him to kiss her. But he wouldn't. He believed getting involved with her would put this case at risk. "He might have talked to someone in jail. Or he might have had a visitor. I want to know everything about the time he was in custody."

Carey took a sip of her coffee, the hot liquid warming her. Coffee would make her feel normal and would help her think. "Why do you care about an innocent man's visitors in jail?"

Reilly started the car. "I'm not sure he's innocent."

Carey stilled, her eyes darting to Reilly. "You think they had the right guy?"

"A hunch tells me we did."

A sick feeling settled over her, her half-eaten bagel sitting like lead in her stomach. "How did he commit another murder while he was in custody?"

"I don't know yet."

"Don't you think Vanessa would have already checked the visitor log?"

Reilly reached into his pocket and handed her his phone. "She wouldn't have had a reason to check it. As far as she knows, she had the wrong person. Can you call Harris and put the phone on speaker?"

Carey set her cup in the holder in front of her. She dialed Harris's cell phone number.

Harris answered on the second ring. "Hey man, we were worried about you guys. The news was talking about another Vagabond Killer murder and how they released the guy they had in custody. Are you both okay?"

Reilly filled Harris in on what had happened in the last twelve hours.

"I think they had the right guy. I think someone else committed that murder."

Harris blew out his breath. "They wouldn't have let the guy go unless they had strong evidence it was the same killer in each case."

"What if the Vagabond Killer told someone how he commits his murders?" Reilly asked.

Startled, Carey's gaze swerved to Reilly's face. If the Vagabond Killer told anyone his secrets, who would be deranged enough to go on a killing spree?

"Assume he did tell someone. That person would have to be willing to kill in the same manner as the Vagabond Killer, same signature," Harris said, his voice indicating he was considering it an option. "Generally, serial killers work alone and they keep their crimes separate from their life. For this guy to commit as many murders as he did without getting caught, he's smart and he doesn't say or do anything in his life to indicate he has these compulsive tendencies. For him to tell someone about them, he took a big leap."

The information swamped her, lighting the fear in her stomach. The killer was out there somewhere, maybe looking for her.

"I need you to find out what you can about Mark Sheffield. He took over Croswell Leone's enterprise after the man died."

"His relationship to Carey is what?"

Carey cringed.

Reilly needed his family's help. They could be trusted. "Mark Sheffield is the man she's running from and Croswell Leone was her father."

"So we're dealing with some seriously dangerous people," Harris said.

Misery and embarassment streamed through her.

"It's good we know who we're up against," Reilly said.

Reilly's phone beeped twice. "Harris, I need to take another call. Let me know if you think of anything else that might be helpful."

Reilly motioned Carey to flip his phone to the other call, and an angry voice started before Reilly could give a greeting.

"Where have you been? Are you with the girl?" The lieutenant's voice shook with anger.

Carey's nerves tensed.

"Yes, I'm with Carey Smith. Things have been hectic."

"Get your butts down here now. I want her in protective custody. The mayor is furious for our incompetence and the media is having a field day with this."

"Respectfully, sir, she is in protective custody. I'm in the best position to watch over Ms. Smith."

Surprise streamed through her. Reilly had had a chance to pass her off to someone else and he hadn't. Her heart soared.

The lieutenant sputtered. "You were almost shot last night. Vanessa told me what happened."

"Neither of us was injured."

Reilly glanced at Carey and she self-consciously touched her face where a few scratches were. In the last month, she'd been battered more than she ever had in her life.

"Where are you now?" the lieutenant asked.

"I'm looking for a safe place to hide the witness," Reilly said.

"I don't have time for games. I need a status. I need to keep track of the witness."

"I'll let you know when I have a safe place to stay."

Was any place safe?

"I've got the mayor riding me on this. This is a total screwup. Get down here now. I won't stand—"

Reilly disconnected the call. "I don't care what the mayor's agenda is. I don't have time for that."

"Reilly!" Carey protested. They had enough trouble with Mark and the Vagabond Killer without adding the rage of an angry lieutenant to their list.

"If I take you to the DPD, Mark might be waiting. Or the media. And if they assign you other protection, will you trust them enough to tell them about Mark? Will you lay it out so it's clear what you're up against?"

She was putting Reilly in a difficult position, pinning him between her and his job. But in truth, it had been a leap for her to tell him about Mark. She wouldn't trust a stranger. "No. I can't tell anyone else."

"Then I'm not going anywhere."

Chapter 10

Carey drank the last of her cold coffee, needing something to do with her hands. Reilly had arranged to meet an old friend at Crestmoor Park. His friend worked in the detention center where the Vagabond Killer had been held.

Would his friend have any evidence to support the theory that they'd had the right man all along? Apprehension swept over her.

They parked in the half-full lot. Carey stuck close to Reilly's side as they made their way toward the walking trail surrounding the park. His arm brushed hers and desire streamed through her. She resisted the impulse to press herself against him or reach for his hand. Her heart skipped a few beats, nervous energy tightening her muscles.

At the start of the trail, a gray haired man in jeans and a flannel jacket stood from a wooden bench and approached them. He and Reilly shook hands.

Reilly introduced her. "Brent, this is Carey Smith. Carey, this is a friend of mine from the police academy."

Carey and Brent shook hands and the three of them walked along the well-worn trail. Reilly stayed close to her, his stance protective.

"You had the alleged Vagabond Killer housed at the detention center," Reilly said, heavy emphasis on the word *alleged*.

Brent tucked his thumbs in the front pockets of his jeans. "I knew him. Crazy son of a gun. Sat in his cell in some kind of meditation pose, mouthing words to himself. If he was sent to trial, I'd guess his lawyer would claim mental insanity. He sure was acting like he had problems."

"Did he make friends with anyone?" Reilly asked. "Did he talk to any of the guards or other prisoners?"

Carey hung on to every word.

Brent shook his head. "Word got around who he was, and by the way he behaved the other prisoners left him alone. They knew he was a short-timer. He was only being held until trial. If he was convicted, he'd be sent to a maximum security prison."

Brent glanced at Carey. "You look familiar. Do I know you?"

Carey squelched the bubble of hysteria that rumbled in her chest. Could she trust Brent with the truth? If word got out that she and Reilly had spoken with someone in Denver, Mark would be hot on her tail.

Recognition lit in Brent's eyes. He snapped his fingers. "I know who you are. You're the woman from the news. You stopped him from killing someone."

A surge of panic flared in Carey's stomach. She instinctively leaned closer to Reilly, wanting his protection and his reassurance she would be okay now that she'd been recognized.

"We're trying to lay low," Reilly said, setting his hand on her lower back. Heat from his touch shimmered up her body. She wanted to bury her face into his shoulder, to let Reilly handle this situation.

Brent nodded. "I got you. I won't say a word."

Reilly lowered his voice. "Did you bring the visitor logs?"

Brent nodded once. "No one can know where you received these. This is unofficial at best."

"Understood," Reilly said.

They stopped on the trail. Brent extended his hand to Reilly and shook it. Carey saw a white slip of paper moving from Brent's hand to Reilly's. Reilly made the paper disappear into his pocket. "We'll get together soon for a beer."

"Sounds great," Brent said.

They said goodbye and Brent continued down the trail in the opposite direction from where they'd met.

Reilly and Carey hiked toward the car.

"You okay?" Reilly asked, glancing at her. He brushed his hand lightly over her cheek where she had a few scratches, frowning mightily at them.

This whole situation made her nervous. "I'm fine. I'm a little rattled that he recognized me. I thought the hair and clothes were a good disguise."

"Brent works in law enforcement and we were asking him about the case. He's trained to notice details and he had time to study you."

Reilly reached for her hand, clasping it in his. Whether it was intentional or a subconscious move to soothe her, she liked when he touched her. It forced away some of the tension wound tight in her muscles, heat infusing her body. Her insides clutched with yearning. Every moment with Reilly was precious and limited. Didn't he see that?

He squeezed her hand. "I'll keep you safe. Just relax."

Her thoughts turned to the visitor log. She inhaled sharply as realization dawned. "You're hoping Mark visited the Vagabond Killer, aren't you?"

Acknowledgment flickered in his eyes. "Or any name that jumps out at you from your past life. Maybe an associate of Mark's, someone who would be willing to help the Vagabond Killer," Reilly said. He rubbed a slow circle with his thumb against her hand. The gesture tossed her train of thought off track, sending her heart skittering against her ribs. "Have I told you how much I like the new hair color?"

No, he hadn't. She patted her hair. "Better than the red?"

"Much." For a moment, his gaze switched to her mouth and she knew he was thinking about kissing her. Thinking about it and trying to talk himself out of it.

When they reached the parking lot, they lowered their heads to avoid eye contact with a couple entering the park.

Inside the car, Reilly said nothing as he pulled from the parking lot and onto the main road. Only then did he reach into his pocket and remove the scrap Brent had given him. He handed it to Carey, one eye on the road, one eye on her.

She unfolded the paper. It was a quarter sheet of paper, with two names written on it. "It's the names of the Vagabond Killer's visitors." The first was Thomas Hartle, Esquire. The second name was Mark Connors. Carey's chest tightened. One of the aliases Mark used.

Her hands trembled and her voice shook. "It's Mark. You were right. He visited the Vagabond Killer."

Tension pulsed off Reilly in waves. "How did Mark get in to see him without throwing up any red flags?"

Another show of Mark's power and extensive reach. "Mark has money and resources to bribe or build a cover. If he wanted to get into the detention center, he would have paid whoever he had to pay or lied to whoever he had to lie."

Why had Mark visited the Vagabond Killer? Did they have anything in common besides the fact that they were both killers and each had reasons for wanting her dead?

A cold shiver ran down her spine. Mark was a silver-tongued negotiator. If he wanted information, he would get it one way or another. Carey reached for Reilly's hand, needing his strength. His hand tightened around hers.

"They planned this together. Mark found a way to get the Vagabond Killer out," Reilly said. "But why? The killer doesn't know where you are. What does Mark gain by setting the killer free?"

Her mouth went dry and her heart pounded hard. She knew Mark. "When I show up dead, he gets the perfect person to pin my murder on."

"Holiday shoppers," Reilly said as they walked toward the front of the superstore. "We'll blend right in." He handed Carey the generic blue wool cap he had picked up at the gas station. She wound her hair to the top of her head and plunked the hat on top of it as he put on his generic red one. He wasn't worried about being followed to the superstore—he'd been careful about doubling back and watching closely—but he couldn't take the chance that someone would recognize either of them.

Carey got out of the rental car. "I'm desperate for some clean clothes." She plucked at her rumpled T-shirt.

Though the shirt was neither tight nor revealing, she looked like a knockout in it. Maybe because he knew what was beneath it. A thought that haunted him more than it should have. His libido was overriding good sense. The impulse to take her, right here, right now, was intense. Would he be able to make it another night lying next to her without kissing her? Without making love with her? He had good reasons not to touch her, not to destroy the case they were building, but those reasons wouldn't quell the longing to hold her.

Reilly forced his mind to their immediate concerns. They both needed fresh clothes. Their overnight into the city had turned into a much longer stay. "Keep your head down and keep close."

Without anyone recognizing them, they could pretend to be a couple and he could keep her close. Hand in hand, fingers interlaced, they walked to the entrance of the store where a blast of hot air and Christmas music greeted them. Carey's hand in his felt good; it felt natural. But it was part of their cover. He wouldn't allow it to lead to anything else.

With so many people taking care of last-minute shopping, Reilly stuck to the middle of the crowd, staying behind other people. He grabbed one of the last carts from the corral and headed in the direction of ladies' clothes.

Carey picked a pair of jeans, two zip-up sweatshirts and two long sleeved T-shirts. As they approached the lingerie department, she glanced at him. "Why don't you head to men's clothes while I pick up a few things?"

Reilly shook his head, keeping his voice low. "This isn't a time to be modest. I'm not leaving you alone."

Because he knew she was embarrassed, he didn't say a word when she threw a pair of pink panties into the basket. His body had its own comment, his stomach tightening and images of her parading around in them flashing through his mind. She tossed in a few more pairs, burying them beneath the jeans and T-shirts. He couldn't stop himself from picturing her wearing the panties. Them and nothing else.

Although after the way he'd behaved, he might not get another chance with her after this case was closed. Did she understand he was doing his best to protect her and trying to keep his head where it should be, focused on the case?

Getting control of his lust, he selected some things from the men's department and they moved on to the personal care section. Wandering up and down the aisles, they each tossed in a few items—soap, shampoo, razors. Carey lingered near the bath products, running her fingertips over the bottles. They held her attention for a few beats and then she shook her head, as if telling herself she couldn't have them. As he walked past, he added them to the cart.

He picked up two disposable, pre-paid cell phones. If Mark had hacked Vanessa's phone, he could hack into Reilly's. Though his phone was supposed to be safe, Reilly didn't trust it. The more connections he cut, the better.

At the end of the aisle, Carey froze and spun around, her eyes wide and her chest rising and falling fast.

"What's the matter?" he asked, alarm pricking at his brain.

"I thought I saw Mark."

Reilly pushed her behind him, peering around the corner. No one was harming her on his watch. "Thought? Or you did?"

"Thought. He looked the same from the back, but when he turned around, it was someone else." Reilly faced her and Carey shook her head, massaging her temples. "I've got to calm down. I'm seeing things."

Reilly rubbed her arms, concentrating on comforting her and ignoring the pang of desire that struck him. "We'll get out of these crowds soon, okay?"

Carey nodded, but she quaked with fear. Would she ever feel safe? Reilly wanted to make her feel better, but he didn't honestly know how safe they were anywhere. Mark had proven to have a long reach.

Reilly's resolve to give her back her life strengthened. She couldn't continue to live this way.

They waited in line for close to an hour to pay for their purchases, keeping their faces forward, heads down. While the waiting was tedious, the frazzled cashier would never remember them. Reilly paid for their items with cash and they collected their bags from the turntable.

"Thank you," Carey said to Reilly as they headed to the car, nodding toward the bags. "I'll pay you back."

Reilly shook his head. "Consider it a Christmas gift."

She smiled at him. "Thank you." The word was spoken with genuine gratitude and he wished he had had time to get her a real gift. If a few necessities made her happy, how would she feel about jewelry or—

Whoa, jewelry? Where had that come from? Jewelry was a gift for a girlfriend. He was trying to keep boundaries defined, not blur them and ruin the case. First, he'd take care of the Vagabond Killer and Mark. Then, he'd take care of Carey.

Hiking to the end of the lot where they had parked the rental, they threw their bags into the backseat of the car. They climbed inside and Reilly turned on the engine and heater. He rifled through the bags, found the prepaid cell phone he'd bought, and plugged one into the car to charge the battery. He powered it on and dialed Vanessa, wanting an update on the situation.

"I've been trying to call you. I even tried calling your parents' place. Where have you been?" she asked.

"I shut off my phone." He wasn't taking any unnecessary chances. "Did you get your phone wiped?"

Vanessa blew out her breath. "Yes, the IT guys gave me a new one and confirmed there was spyware on my other one. How am I supposed to get messages to you if you're not going to answer?"

"Leave me a voice mail. I'll check them from time to time."

Vanessa harrumphed. "Fine. I was trying to call you about the suspect we had in custody, John Sundry. After we released him, we kept a couple of tails on him, just in case. He lost them." A tremor of fear ran through Vanessa's voice.

Reilly gripped the steering wheel, tension knotting in his shoulders. "When? How?"

"This afternoon. Sundry went into a diner and never came out. They searched high and low. He's in the wind," Vanessa said.

Reilly swore inwardly. "Are you somewhere safe?"

"The lieutenant insisted I stay with him and his wife. Anyone closely connected to the case has been put on alert. Do you think we made a mistake? Do you think we had the right guy?"

"Men with nothing to hide don't run." After his visit with Brent, Reilly was doubly convinced they'd had the right man and he'd been sprung with evidence manufactured by Mark.

He heard Vanessa drumming her fingers on something hard. "I'll call if anything changes. Be careful out there." A touch of warmth tinged her voice.

"You do the same."

He disconnected the call and looked at Carey. She waited for him to speak, her eyes wide. "Something happened. Please, tell me quickly."

He hated delivering more bad news. "They had a tail on John Sundry, the man they had arrested as being the Vagabond Killer. They lost him."

Carey wrapped her arms around her midsection as if trying to hold herself together. "He's coming for me, isn't he?"

Not if Reilly had any say in the matter. "He has to find you first." And it was his job to make that impossible.

They traveled away from the city, searching for lodging, any safe place for them to stay. They were turned away by three hotels before they found one with a vacancy. The hotel was six stories high, the windows facing the front lined with garland. Green wreaths with red bows decorated them and trees trimmed with gold garland and shimmering Christmas ornaments filled the lobby.

Reilly checked in and they took the elevator to the third floor. They needed to rest, and weariness was showing on Carey's face.

He called Harris on his cell and when he didn't answer, Reilly left the number to one of the cell phones. Then he tucked it in his pocket, flopped on the bed and listened to the sound of children tearing up and down the hallway, their hotel room doors slamming, parents commanding them to be quiet, and giggles of excitement drifting under their door.

The sound brought back memories of his childhood Christmases.

Carey rifled through her duffel and pulled out her toothbrush and toothpaste. "I'm going to get ready for bed." She flipped her dark hair over her shoulder and gave him a small smile.

The urge to go to her and band his arms around her torpedoed through him. "You okay?" he asked, hearing something resonate in her voice.

She looked at the carpet. "Christmas makes me miss my father."

Reilly swung his feet to the floor and gestured for her to come closer. She crossed the room and sat on his knee, resting her head on his shoulder. Tenderness crackled in the space between them.

"I know you think he was a bad man, but to me he wasn't a criminal. He was my dad." She wiped away a tear with her finger. "He took good care of me. After my mom left us, he had to be both parents and he didn't let me down. He came to my school events and he helped me with my homework." She swallowed hard. "It's hard to be alone."

Reilly slipped his arms around her. "You aren't alone. We're together."

She bit her lip and brought her hand to his hair, running her fingers through it, pushing it away from his face. The gentleness of her touch ignited heat in his body.

"You should go to your parents' ranch and be with your family for the holiday. Your brothers came home so you could be together," she said.

Reilly read the sadness in her eyes, the guilt swimming there. He had committed to her and he was staying the course. "I told you. I'm not abandoning you."

She looked away from him. "I'm sorry for this. I don't know what to do next. Do you hear those children?" She pointed toward the door.

"Kinda hard not to. Do you want me to ask them to be quiet?" He didn't mind their laughter, but she was under a lot of stress. Maybe it was grating her.

"No. They aren't bothering me. They're having fun. They're with their families. I'll never get to have that. I'll never have a baby to hold in my arms or a husband who comes home to me at night. The best I can hope for is to find people to spend a holiday or two with before I have to change cities." Her voice cracked and she covered her face with her hands.

He gathered her close and stroked her hair. Her shoulders shook, wracked by sobs. "It's going to be okay. We're going to find the Vagabond Killer and we're going to find Mark. You'll have those things."

He could picture her as a mother, fierce and protective, yet willing to let her children explore. And in that picture, he could see himself beside her.

The realization caught him off guard. Why was he thinking about these things? The holiday getting to him? Or her? Was she getting to him? He'd hoped they'd have a future, at some point after this case was over, but the permanence of his vision startled him.

Her breath heated his shoulder in uneven puffs. "I'm getting too emotional because I'm tired. I'll be okay." She spoke the words but made no attempt to move away. "I think you should go back to the ranch for the holiday."

He struggled with half a mind to push her away and half a mind to never let her go. "I'm sure they'd love to have both of us there." He wanted her with him.

She sniffed and wiped at her eyes. "How can you be sure we won't be followed? Or that Mark isn't waiting for us there?"

"We've zigzagged too much. No one has been following us. My dad would have called if anyone was on the property."

She relaxed infinitesimally. "Why don't you call them and talk it over? I'll leave you alone and get ready for bed. I won't hold you to anything."

Reilly leaned away and looked at her. It saddened him that she expected people—him in particular—to let her down. "I have a little surprise for you."

She inclined her head. "What kind of surprise? Last few weeks, my surprises have been bad ones."

He shifted her to the bed and went to the pile of superstore plastic bags. Searching through them, he found what he was looking for and lifted the bag in triumph. "Bubble bath and bath salts."

She smiled through her tears, a beautiful sight. "How did you know I wanted them?"

She *had* wanted them. It pleased him he'd been right in reading her reaction. "I saw you eyeing them. And my mom loves things like that, so I figured you could use a little pampering. It's not much…"

Carey took the bag from him and reached her free hand to the back of his neck. She pulled his face to hers, their noses brushing against each other. "Thank you for this. Thank you for everything you've done. You're—" she paused, as if searching for the words "—you're an amazing man."

"You're welcome," he said, electricity shooting between them.

Pulling on his neck, she pressed his mouth flush to hers, her lips tickling his. She dropped the bag to the floor and brought both hands around his neck, anchoring herself to him.

He'd wanted to put off thoughts of the future to some later point, but he couldn't seem to keep them from popping into his head. Whenever he'd tried to resist her, he'd failed. Deep down, she was who he wanted. Why was he denying it? Why was he pushing her away?

She meant more to him than a linchpin holding together a case.

Her inability to believe she had a future, made her believe they had only now. He'd show her they had now and they had later.

Her mouth opened beneath his and he tasted her, mint and coffee. Deep kisses, hard kisses, soft kisses, his mouth explored hers. It had been too long since he had kissed her, since she had been in his arms. His hands hummed with pleasure as he slid them from her hips to her lower back, molding her against his body.

The boundaries he'd constructed took one final blow and then tumbled down. Denial hadn't worked and trying to put his feelings on hold had transformed his hunger into starvation. He sensed her need, her hunger as deep as his own, and his body responded to it. He was no longer a detective protecting a witness; he was a man protecting his woman. This time, he wouldn't sneak away or let worry and fear control him. This time, he was promising her a future. A future with him.

He could only think about her, her body pressed into his, her lips brushing his, her scent invading his nostrils. She intoxicated him. At this moment he never wanted to be separated from her.

A small sigh sounded in the back of her throat, escalating his excitement, heating the air around them to a sizzle and burn. She pushed her hips against his. Her hands slipped from his neck to his chest, her fingertips pressing into his flesh, searing him with her heat, her intensity.

Every time they came together, heat and lightning exploded between them. He took a step toward the bed and she moved with him, her thigh brushing his, fire whipping up his body. Two more steps and a small shove from her and his back hit the bed, his arms pulling her down. Her hair created a curtain around them as she held herself over him.

"Reilly."

"Hmmm?"

"Your pocket is vibrating."

He didn't care about the phone. "Ignore it. It will stop."

He ran his hand along the waistband of her pants, touching the blazing skin of her midsection. Her skin was soft, her breasts pressing into his hard chest. The vibrating phone stopped. He reached for the hem of her shirt to peel it over her head. The phone vibrated again.

Lifting his head and groaning, he rolled her to the side. He wanted to fling the phone away. He didn't want to answer. He didn't want to know whatever news would be delivered or answer whatever questions were going to be asked.

"It might be important," she said, her voice soft, even as her fingers trailed down his thigh.

He dug in his pocket for the prepaid phone, Harris's number lighting on the display. Taking a deep breath, he answered.

Carey got out of bed, picking the plastic bag containing her bubble bath off the floor. She swung it on her finger and went into the bathroom, winking, and then closed the door behind her.

"Did I wake you? You sound like you were sleeping," Harris said.

Sleeping...in the throes of passion. Whatever. "It's been a rough couple of days."

"We've managed to dig up some information and compile a few theories."

His family was a brain trust of information about criminals. He would bet they'd had hours of conversation, debating Mark's psyche and the Vagabond Killer's next move. "Anything you have will help. We don't know where either Mark or John Sundry are."

Harris blew out his breath in a huff. "They released Sundry and didn't put a tail on him?"

"He shook the tail. No one's seen him since this morning."

"Are you somewhere safe?"

"Relatively."

"Come home. You're safest here," Harris said.

Carey hadn't seemed convinced it was the best option, but she didn't know his family as well as he did. They were safest watching each other's backs. "We will. Soon," Reilly said. He was on limited minutes and he wanted the information Harris had gathered. "What did you come up with?"

"We couldn't find a link between them prior to John Sundry being held in jail. But Mark has a long history of run-ins with the law, all of them resulting in him coming up blameless of any wrongdoing."

Reilly snorted. "How many palms did he grease for that fortuitous result?"

"More than I want to think about," Harris said. "I've brought a few inconsistencies to the attention of the right people, people we can trust to do the right thing." Harris cleared his throat. "Haley Leone has been missing in action for nearly a year. She doesn't have any pending warrants for her arrest, but she's listed as a missing person and a person of interest in several cases involving both her father, deceased, and Mark Sheffield."

Not what he wanted to hear. He'd wanted Carey to come back innocent of any wrongdoing. "She admitted she knows things about Mark. She's too afraid to spill them."

"If she's willing to come forward, we can make a case that she acted under duress, and taking into account her clean record and her father's death, I think the D.A. would agree her fleeing was for her own protection."

Reilly wanted to abscond with her, to keep her safe and prevent any of the difficulties that were coming her way. "What about John Sundry? Any history?"

Reilly heard Harris clicking at his computer. "From the age of four, he was in the foster-care system. Most of those records are sealed, but we can assume he was another lost child. He served a brief stint in the military, dishonorably discharged for going MIA in battle."

"Does that fit the profile? He kills people. Why avoid conflict in wartime?"

Harris typed some more. "He attacks people weaker than he is. An opponent pointing a gun at him would terrify him. He needs the violence to sate his anger, but he won't attack someone he perceives as stronger."

"Deep down he's a coward," Reilly said. He could have guessed as much about Sundry. "What's the likelihood he'll come after Carey?"

"That's where my profile gets speculative. He would view her as strong, since she survived an altercation with him. In my opinion there's a good chance he's formed an obsession with her."

Reilly let go a curse. He'd known the situation was

difficult, but a serial killer and a crime lord with an obsession with Carey? Worst kind of attention.

"Come home. Dad had one of his SEAL buddies here arming the house with more firepower, configuring the security system and making the safe house strong enough to withstand a nuclear holocaust. Mom's been worried sick. You can't stay awake around the clock and Carey isn't trained to protect herself. I know you're worried about luring them here, but the alternative is that we come to you. We've got to circle the wagons."

Circle the wagons. It was their family's war cry when one of them was at risk. Get close and stay close. Watch each other's backs. Harris was right. "I'm going to get some sleep. We'll head for the ranch first thing in the morning."

"Call if you need anything," Harris said, relief evident in his voice.

"Will do. Give my love to everyone."

They disconnected the call and Reilly silenced the prepaid phone then laid it on the dresser. He didn't want any more distractions. For the next six to eight hours, he was alone in this hotel room with Carey. The kisses they'd shared lingered on his mind. Denying his attraction to her and pretending he could wait had only made desire throb harder in his veins. Make the best use of now. Live for the moment. Make her see how good the future could be. The idea of taking Carey in his arms was more than he could resist.

Beautiful Carey, currently lying naked in the bathtub.

Chapter 11

Reilly heard gentle splashes of Carey in the bathtub. Taking the lead from their kiss and fully intending to pick up where they'd been before his brother's call, he knocked on the door to the bathroom.

"Come in," she said, her voice warm and inviting.

He opened the door and stepped inside. The steam of her bath had fogged the mirror. She was hidden beneath the white iridescent bubbles.

"Looks like you're having fun," he said. He was barely holding on to his self-control, his body completely aroused.

She lifted her head from the tub where she'd been reclining, a towel rolled under her neck. "It's been close to a year since I've had a bubble bath. The bathtub in my apartment never felt clean enough for a soak." Hot water dripped into the tub from the faucet.

His eyes roamed across her face and then skittered

across the bubbles. The scent of the bath, floral and spicy, floated in the air. Lust wound tight inside him.

Entering this bathroom was crossing a line. It was a step he was ready to make. To put his concerns as a detective aside to try to give her a sense of safety and security in him as a man.

She could count on him completely. He needed her to believe that and to believe in the future. His career came second to her. Second to her needs.

"Everything okay with your family?" she asked. "You're looking at me strangely." She looked down and moved the bubbles around, checking that she was covered.

Reilly knelt on the floor next to the tub. "You're beautiful."

"Thank you."

"It's not just a compliment. You're beautiful and smart and caring. You deserve to have an amazing life."

She shifted. "I don't know where you're going with this, but I get it. You don't have to soften the rejection with compliments. I know we have to have boundaries and that kiss wasn't supposed to happen. We can leave it at a kiss. It doesn't have to happen again."

She wasn't getting it. He was going to show her. "I want it to happen again. The first moment I saw you, the night you came running out of the alley, my first instinct was to get to you and hold you. I wanted you. I pride myself on being professional and distant. But with you, that was impossible. I want you, Carey, and I'm tired of fighting it."

Her eyes blazed into his. "Would you like to join me?" she asked almost shyly.

Her invitation was irresistible. He peeled his shirt over his head and tossed it to the ground. She was pure temptation and a deep, burning need seared him. He wouldn't let the case stand between him and Carey, not anymore. He was lying to himself, pretending they had slept together once and it had been a mistake that was easily forgotten. What they had together had grown beyond lineups, a protector-witness relationship and a one-night fling. They had now and they had a future. He was staking his bets on it.

Carey flicked some water on him and grinned. "Come on in, the water's fine."

Carey knew the sacrifice he was making. He was putting her first, ahead of his career. When had anyone put her first? It felt amazing. In that moment she felt cherished and cared for.

"Where's the phone?" she asked.

"Silenced in the other room."

No distractions. No interruptions. She wanted Reilly to herself. "Get in."

Carey shifted in the tub making room for him to slide in behind her. Stripping off the last of his clothes, he stepped into the tub and brought the other foot over the ledge. He sat behind her, extending his legs around her body.

She relaxed against him, resting her head against his chest. "Doesn't this feel nice?"

He ran his hands over her belly, pushing aside the bubbles and cupping her breasts in his hands. His arousal pressed into her back. "Very nice."

She giggled and set her hand on his thighs, squeezing them, her nails scraping lightly. "You have to get clean before we play."

"I'd rather play and then get clean."

She didn't want to rush. Not tonight. They were alone

in a hotel room, and if they were lucky, they had an entire night together. She wanted him; she wanted this. For the first time in over eleven months, when she closed her eyes and thought of the future, she could see something besides crappy jobs and lonely apartments. She could see Reilly in the near future, spending Christmas with him, and in the distant future, spending her life with him.

She'd never allowed herself the luxury of imagining before. Not with Mark looking for her. Not with the past chasing her. Carey shut down those destructive thoughts. Whatever was going to happen with Mark, he wouldn't terrorize her tonight. Not tonight.

Carey took the blue bar of soap from the ledge and rubbed it between her hands. Then she ran it over Reilly's arms and legs, working the soap into bubbles while she massaged his taut muscles. As she turned in his arms, water rushed from her body into the tub and she rose from the bubbles, kneeling in front of him.

"Your muscles are tight. Are you nervous?" she asked. She didn't want him to be. She wanted him to be as calm as she was. Though they'd made love before, something about this time was different. The trust and honesty between them made the connection stronger, deeper.

"Not nervous," he said, his gaze heated. "Excited."

She moved the soap around his neck and chest, rinsing him with the hot water from the tub. As her hands lathered the soap on his skin, Reilly clasped her waist, fire blazing from his touch. The contact burned her to her core. Her hand moved beneath the water and skimmed between his legs, closing over him. He bucked against her hand.

Her breath escaped on a whispered sigh. She slid her

hand over him and he shifted his body, reaching for her and sending a finger inside her.

She closed her eyes and let her head fall back, her grip on him loosening. New tides of anticipation flooded her.

Reilly stood and pulled her to her feet, flicking the drain open and turning on the shower. A quick blast of cold, followed by steaming hot water poured over them.

He pressed her against the tile of the shower and she gasped. Her ribs still ached when she moved in certain ways, but what Reilly was doing to her felt so good her injuries became a distant memory. "It's cold."

"Give me a chance to make it hot." He nuzzled her neck and brought his mouth to hers, kissing her indulgently, deeply, his tongue stroking hers, building their pleasure until she couldn't think about anything except the electric press of skin against skin and her body melting into his.

He parted her thighs, lifting her foot and setting it on the ledge of the tub. His body was in line with hers and he was ready. He paused. "I need a minute."

He kissed her hard and got out of the tub. Her legs quaked and she gripped the shower head to maintain her balance. He returned in a moment, foil packet in hand.

Carey waited with growing anticipation. Sheathing himself, he reached between her legs and ran his finger along the apex of her thighs. She needed this. She needed him. She was hot and ready, and she moved her hips against him in invitation.

He reached to her lower back and pulled her body against him, capturing her mouth with his in a slow, deep kiss. He tasted of mint and smelled of spice. Fresh and masculine, both calming her and arousing her at once.

He positioned himself between her legs. The need was overpowering. Slowing down was impossible. In one smooth motion, he buried himself inside her. She cried out, her fingernails digging into his shoulder blades. He moved out and in, out and in, pleasure building in her core. Excitement escalated inside her and she grasped his hips, urging him faster. He cupped under her buttocks, lifting her into his arms, sliding her against him and creating the perfect friction between their bodies. Their wet mouths slipped together, their tongues stroking, tasting. They fit perfectly as he pushed into her. Wrapping her arms around him, she accepted him as a part of her.

With insistent, powerful thrusts, he pumped into her, faster, deeper, until she found release in his arms. She cried out his name and moments later he exploded inside her, moving slower as her climax eased. Incredible. The power of their love-making made her body quiver.

He set her feet on the tub and disposed of the condom, letting the water ripple over their bodies.

She waited to feel sadness at the idea it was the last time. None came. No sense of loss hit her. This wasn't a mistake. This was good. This was right. For the first time, they were on the same page, in this together, without secrets between them.

Reilly had given her the fragile, delicate hope that she could leave the past behind her and start over fresh.

A new life. A clean start.

Hope. Wonderful hope. Only the knowledge that Mark was out there, still looking for her, threatened to destroy it.

Carey slept curled next to him, her back pressed to his chest, her hips nestled into the curve of his body.

Reilly let his hand drift along her side. He had missed having this connection with someone. The children running through the halls had settled around 10:00 p.m. and with Carey's warm body tucked against him, it had been easy to drift off to sleep for a couple of hours. He woke several times throughout the night, once when a door slammed in the hallway, alert to anyone approaching their room.

Lying in the dark, he worked his mind over the ways Mark or John Sundry could trace them. Reilly had checked into the hotel using cash and a hefty deposit. Few people had seen him and Carey together, and they'd changed locations twice since the attack at the police station. The hotel was filled with harried holiday travelers, making it easy to blend. He wasn't driving his car and the rental could belong to any number of visitors.

But he wasn't going to get too comfortable. He'd underestimated Mark before and had nearly paid for it with his and Carey's lives. They needed to keep moving, make sure they weren't followed, and get somewhere safe.

Reilly was accustomed to going with five or six hours' sleep and a few naps in between shifts. Crimes he worked haunted him, making his thoughts race and chasing away sleep. This one was no different, except that he had the witness with him in his arms. He was responsible for keeping her safe. He rolled onto his back, stared at the ceiling, trying to force his mind to slow enough to sleep another hour.

Carey let out a contented sigh and shifted, slipping her arm around his waist. He drew her against him and a sense of utter peace fell over him. He couldn't put his finger on the precise moment his feelings for her had changed. She wasn't just a witness in a case he was working. She was someone he wanted in his life for more than the present. He wanted her for keeps.

Chapter 12

"You're just in time," Jane said as Carey and Reilly came through the front door, stomping their boots on the welcome mat to bang off the snow.

Carey inhaled the scent of freshly baked cookies and her stomach growled. They'd taken a longer, indirect route, Reilly's concern about being followed ever present, and they'd stopped only once for gas and snacks.

Reilly unwound the scarf from his neck. "In time for what?"

"We're trimming the Christmas tree," Jane said, taking their coats.

Brady appeared in the hallway, holding a mug in his hand. "You missed the hard part. Mom made us chop down a tree from the woods and haul it in here."

"Tradition," Jane said, turning to Carey. "Did your family chop down a Christmas tree every year?"

Carey shook her head. "No, we hired people to come

to the house to decorate and trim the tree." Those same people wrapped garland around the banisters and laid it on the mantle, leaving the house scented in pine and glimmering with lights and glitter. Soon after Christmas, they returned to take away the decorations, vacuuming and wiping up every last bit of sparkle.

"Maybe you'll get a chance to help us next year," Jane said.

Optimistic. Possible. That fragile hope that Reilly had instilled in her cried out with joy. Carey was quick to temper it. She would take it day by day.

"I've fixed some snacks and we're getting ready to put the balls on the tree. Do you want to help?" Jane asked.

Carey glanced at Reilly, unsure if she should beg off and leave his family to their traditions. He nodded once and smiled at her as if to say, "I want you to join us."

Carey's heart warmed in her chest. "That sounds like fun."

She followed Jane to the living room where Doc was holding the tree by the trunk and Harris was beneath it, affixing the stand.

Jane knelt by a red plastic container with a green lid, popping the sides open and lifting it. The inside was filled with colored ornaments, red, green, gold and silver. Jane hooked a few ornaments and carried them to the tree. Reilly turned on Christmas music, playing it low.

Carey was unsure of where she fit in here. Everyone else seemed to have a role. She was the outsider.

Reilly motioned for her to come over. He handed her an ornament with his name scrawled across it. "I made this in the third grade."

She examined the gingerbread man with silver writing on the front. "That's pretty good handwriting for a boy."

Reilly lifted his brows. "I always was an over-achiever."

Brady snorted. "You mean you've always had girly handwriting."

"You're just jealous because no one can read your writing," Harris said, nudging Brady in the ribs.

Carey listened to their familiar banter and smiled at their teasing. Being an only child with one parent had been lonely at times. She'd never had that warm familiarity with anyone.

Carey walked to the tree and placed the ornament near the center, turning it so Reilly's name faced out. She started when he set his hands on her hips and brought his mouth close to her ear. "Looks great."

Turning, she pushed his shoulders slightly. She felt his family's curious gazes. "I can't take credit for that. I didn't pick the tree and I put on one ornament."

He waggled his eyebrows playfully. "What makes you think I was talking about the tree?"

Her cheeks flushed hot, knowing his family had heard but were pretending they hadn't. Something had changed between her and Reilly in the last few days, their relationship moving to deeper levels, faster than she'd thought possible. His positive outlook had started to rub off on her. She wanted to believe her problems would work out, that Mark and the Vagabond Killer would be caught and jailed and she'd be safe to live her life out in the open— no hiding, no running—with Reilly at her side.

Reilly couldn't keep his eyes off her. Carey was beautiful. He'd thought it from the first moment he'd met her and seeing her with his family felt right. She fit.

He'd tried to ignore the attraction. He'd tried to maintain his distance. But it had been futile. They belonged together.

"Is this a Christmas Eve Truman family tradition?" Carey asked, taking a seat on the floor near the fireplace.

"This and the town Christmas party," Brady said.

Reilly shot his brother a silencing look. Carey had asked about the banner announcing the town's Christmas party as they'd driven in and Reilly had waved off the question. His family attended every year, but they wouldn't this year. Carey would be noticed as an out-of-towner and people would ask questions they didn't want to have to answer.

"It's a small get-together held in the mayor's barn. We weren't planning to attend," Doc said and Reilly mentally thanked his father for knowing he wouldn't want to go.

Carey narrowed her eyes and looked around the room. Everyone refused to make eye contact with her. "Because of me?"

Reilly took her hand, the contact elevating his body temperature and stirring his emotion. He would do anything to protect her. She didn't need to lump more guilt onto herself. Carey's safety was more important than a holiday gathering. "It's safer for us to stay here."

Carey pulled her hand away. "Everyone doesn't need to stay with me. You should go. All of you. I'll be fine here by myself. I'll find a good holiday movie on TV and relax on the couch."

"Absolutely not," Jane said. "We're not leaving you alone on Christmas Eve."

They fell silent except for the sound of the crackling fire.

"Why don't I stay here with Carey and the rest of the family can go?" Reilly asked. A night with Carey wasn't a hardship. He could think of a number of things they could do alone.

Carey frowned. If she knew the ideas racing through his mind, she'd be smiling, agreeing to stay with him. "Then you won't be with your family. I'll be fine alone. I have lots of things I need to catch up on."

"Like?" Reilly asked, knowing she'd be bored and lonely.

Carey glowered at him. "I could paint my nails. Or read a book. Or get some extra sleep."

Reilly wasn't leaving her alone. "I'll stay with you. The rest can go." It was a party. Missing it wasn't a big deal. "Dad has the cameras hooked up and I'll keep the alarms on. We'll be safe."

Doc nodded at his son. "It's your choice."

"We can stop in for a short while, and then we'll come back to the ranch and spend the rest of the evening with you two," Jane said.

Brady and Harris mumbled their agreements. The best of both worlds—time alone with Carey and time with his family. "Carey and I will have fun. Don't worry about us."

"Do you really not mind missing the party?" Carey asked after his family had left with promises they'd return soon.

"A couple of hours alone with you? Better than any party I can think of," Reilly said, sitting next to her on the couch, slipping his arm around her.

The sultry hum of anticipation floated in the air. Alone in a safe place with Reilly. A sense of calm washed over her—everything was going to be okay.

The smell of hot cider drifted from their mugs and the crackling fire warmed the room. This was the best Christmas she'd had in a long while, maybe ever.

Carey brought her mug to her lips and jolted when an alarm rang, sending cider down the front of her. The shrillness of the sound petrified her. In the time she'd been with the Trumans, she'd never heard one of his father's alarms trip.

Terror slammed into her. Mark had truly found her this time.

Reilly was on his feet in moments, setting his cup down and taking her hand. "Monitoring console's in my dad's office. Maybe an animal tripped one of the alarms."

"It's Mark. He's found us." Her legs shaking with fear, she followed Reilly, her hand tucked in his. The smell of smoke wafted through the house. A fire. A chilling sense of panic tore through her.

Reilly must have caught the scent of the fire, too, and raced faster, entering Doc's office and scanning the video monitors and alarms. He flicked a red switch at the console.

Carey looked at the monitors, searching for the source of the problem. Where was the fire? Where was Mark? She didn't see anyone else on the screens, but she knew Mark was out there, somewhere, lying in wait. How could they escape without Mark finding them? Was he inside the house? Or lurking outside in the dark?

Reilly dialed the combination lock on a wall safe and opened it, pulling out two guns. One he slid into his back pocket and the other he palmed in his hand. "I hit the panic button. I want the family back here. The alarm will notify the fire and police departments, as well. I need to get you to the safe house."

"He's going to kill me. He won't leave here until I'm dead."

Reilly shook his head. "He has to get through me first. We're going to be okay." Carey recognized the determination in his eyes. Reilly continued, "Mark can't be everywhere at once. The fire's on the west side of the house. Stay at my side until we get to the safe house under the barn. Once I secure you, do not open the door for anyone. Stay inside until I come get you."

He was already moving and she ran to catch up with him. "Where are you going to be?"

"I'll handle this," Reilly said, his voice tight. "I'll keep you safe."

Could anyone keep her safe? After all the Trumans had done, Mark had found a way to get to her.

The smell of smoke grew thicker in the air. "What are you planning to do?" she asked, straining to speak through the smoke that had replaced oxygen in the room.

Reilly dragged her to her knees and they crawled toward the back door in the kitchen. Even the air near the floor burned her lungs as she inhaled.

"I'm going to get you somewhere safe and then I'm going to end this once and for all." Reilly reached for the dead bolt on the door leading outside and snapped it open. His hand moved to the door handle.

Carey looked out into the dark. "It's not safe out there. We don't know where he is." Did they have a few minutes to wait for the fire department to arrive? As if in response to her silent question, the roar of the fire grew louder, stronger.

Reilly pulled open the door and fresh air invaded her lungs. He helped her to her feet and they rushed to the end of the porch. "I'm doing everything I can, Carey.

Please trust me. We need to run as fast as we can toward the barn. I won't let go of your hand, okay?"

Carey nodded, fear so taut in her throat she couldn't speak.

Snow soaked through her socks as they ran. Reilly was sure on his feet, keeping her standing when hers skidded out from under her. Cold air bit into her lungs and the smell of smoke clung to the air. A few of the outdoor lights were on and the plowed path gave them some guidance in the dark.

The barn was in sight, the light over the door burning bright, beckoning to them. Only ten yards to go. Once they were inside, she would insist Reilly wait with her. She wasn't letting him stash her somewhere safe and then put himself at risk. She wouldn't lose him now. He meant too much to her.

A blast shuddered through the night. The house collapsing under the weight of the fire? What if they had left seconds later? Carey looked over her shoulder and lost her balance, but this time, Reilly didn't keep her upright. Whirling toward him in surprise, she found him kneeling on the ground clutching his shoulder.

"Reilly? What is it?" she asked, straining to see in the light projected from the barn. "We're almost there."

He brought his hand away from his shoulder, his fingers covered in blood. What had happened? What did she need to do to stop the bleeding? "Can you make it the rest of the way?" Could she drag him? Carry him? Did the safe house have bandages for treating injuries?

"Go, Carey. Just go. I'm right behind you."

Hysteria billowed inside her. "No! I'm not leaving you." She bent down at his uninjured side and hefted his arm over her shoulders. "Come on, we're going together."

She struggled to stand under his weight. They made it two steps and then Reilly collapsed. Terror for Reilly clawed at her chest. Where was help? He'd hit the panic button! Kneeling at his side, she pressed her hands over his shoulder to try to stop the blood. Reilly groaned but didn't open his eyes.

"Reilly, please, stay with me. We're going to be fine." She had to believe that. Had to trust help would come.

A hand clamped around her midsection, yanking her to her feet and snapping her forcefully around. Carey's eyes went to her assailant's face, terror clutching her heart, making it impossible to breathe and impossible to scream.

Mark's eyes blazed with rage. She had no doubt in her mind. He was going to kill her.

Chapter 13

Carey had known Mark would never let her get away from him and live. Her world collapsed around her as every nightmare came to life. Reilly was injured. The Trumans' house was destroyed. She'd brought hurt and anguish to the people who had tried to protect her.

Foremost, terror for Reilly's life swamped her. She had to help him. She couldn't leave him in the snow, in the dark, alone. How long before someone found him? What could she do to help him?

Mark's arm locked around her waist. He pressed a gun into her side, hard enough that pain shot up her still fragile ribs. "Hey there, doll. I've been looking for you. Don't scream or I'll open fire on your boyfriend. I don't care who dies as long as you're among them. Although it was amusing to watch you try to help him." Still clasping her to him, Mark reached to Reilly's limp hand and took his gun, throwing it away into the dark.

Fear sent her heart racing and alarm bells shrieking in her mind. She couldn't let Reilly die because of her. She clung to the hope that Reilly was unconscious, not dead, and help was on the way. He couldn't bleed to death. Reilly had to be okay.

If she let Mark take her, would he leave Reilly alone? Reilly's family would be there soon. They would find him and help him.

Mark dragged her away from Reilly, toward the bare fields behind the barn. Is this how it ended for her? Dying at Mark's hands on a cold, dark field? What would keep him from killing her and then going back for Reilly and the Trumans? She closed her eyes and determination filled her chest.

She was not going down without a fight. She was Haley Leone. She was a fighter. A survivor. She'd run away and forgotten who she was—but this is where it stopped. She'd protect the Trumans and herself—or die trying.

She had so much to live for, so much she needed to do. She had to tell Reilly she loved him. She was in love with Reilly Truman. Not having said the words to him and knowing she might never get to say them struck her as deeply unfair. Categorically wrong. A lot of bad things had happened to her in the last year, but this one seemed like the worst.

She stumbled, stalling for time. Mark jerked her upright. "Don't try it. I'll put a bullet in your head and then I'll kill your detective."

Her mind screamed in protest. She wouldn't let that happen. She would find a way out of this without getting Reilly killed.

"You've put me through a lot of trouble," Mark said,

dragging her to an area hidden by the Trumans' barn. "I don't appreciate that."

She took several deep breaths. Trickery? Lies? How would she get away? "Mark, I'm so glad you found me. I've been hiding from the feds."

He threw back his head and let out a sharp bark of laughter. "Nice. You're still a liar. Doesn't matter what load of bull you try to feed me. I can't trust you."

Her mouth was dry, the cold making her eyes water. "Yes, you can. I was trying to protect us by hiding until you got my dad's businesses in the clear and the feds stopped poking around."

"Cut the bull. You know too much and you could put me in prison for a long time. Did you think I would let you live after you ran away?"

She tried again. "I was running for us."

Mark struck her across the face with the back of his hand and released her. The impact sent her reeling. She fell to the ground.

"Stop lying."

Carey tasted blood in her mouth. "You don't have to do this."

"I loved you, Haley. I would have given you a life fit for a queen."

He'd never loved her. He'd loved the things her father had given him, the lifestyle he'd been granted by being associated with her family. Mark was right about the material things he would provide, things bought with money earned from her father's businesses, with dirty, blood money. It made her ill to think about it. She glared up at him. "Everything you do, you do for yourself. You never cared about my father or me. You cared about the money. I've had to give up everything to get away from you. My friends. My family. My home. You hurt me and you hurt the people around me. What about Tracy? Why did you kill her? She didn't have anything to do with why I ran."

Mark's eyes glinted. "She lied to me and she paid for those lies. And now so will you."

Carey had given up her dreams and hopes for the future. Mark didn't deserve to take those things away from her. No one did. She wanted a future with Reilly. She wanted her life back. "You're going to regret what you've done. You're going to regret hurting me."

Was it unreasonable hope or did she hear sirens in the distance? Someone had to find Reilly and help him. She pushed herself to her feet. She needed to protect herself and keep Mark from hurting Reilly further. Was there anything around she could use as a weapon? Why hadn't she thought to ask for a gun when they were in Doc's office?

Mark stepped closer to her. "Letting you live is the only regret I'd have. You brought this on yourself. Look at me, Haley."

He used the barrel of the gun to force her to look at him. She lifted her head slowly, half expecting him to strike her again.

"I'll remember you this way." His hand caressed her cheek and she jerked her head away.

He tsked. "Don't be like that. Not when I went through the trouble of arranging a surprise for you."

The way he said the word *surprise,* she knew he intended to end her life. Should she scream? Even if the police had arrived, would anyone hear her over the noise of the raging fire? Would she draw someone else here, someone Mark would kill? She set her jaw. She wouldn't scream, but given the chance, she'd defend herself. "Are your lackeys here to take care of me? You never could face anyone alone."

Mark smirked at her. "No, this time I have a partner. Didn't even have to hire him. He was more than happy to help me."

The Vagabond Killer stepped from the side of the barn to stand next to Mark. "Hello, Haley. I have dreamt of this moment. I'm John, your savior."

A cold sweat broke out over her body. She recognized his face immediately and the name… John? John Sundry? The Denver police had had the right man in custody. The Vagabond Killer knew her name—her real name. He knew who she was. Fear shook her insides, made her entire body tremble.

"I said hello. The polite thing is for you to reply," John said, anger hot in his voice.

Her vocal chords tightened, yet she managed to force out a word. "Hi."

"Have you missed me?" John asked.

Mark stepped away and Carey had the insane impulse to grab on to him. She knew Mark. He wouldn't hesitate to hurt her or kill her, but he wasn't into torture. The Vagabond Killer had done some ugly, horrifying things to his victims.

Was she next?

"I m-missed you," she croaked out, taking a step away from him.

Mark took a ball of twine from his pocket. "Hands behind your back or I'll shoot you." Ice glinted in his voice. How had she ever thought she loved this man? A man who could kill without mercy?

"No!" John shouted.

Mark turned slowly, his eyebrows raised. "You said you wanted time alone with her."

The Vagabond Killer withdrew his knife. "Don't touch her. She belongs to me. She is the only woman worthy of me."

Carey's eyes darted left and right, looking for a place to run. She was stuck between them; they could catch her fleeing. She would bide her time, waiting for an opening to take off.

"Fine, John. Do whatever you want to her. I'm finished with her." Mark shoved his gun into the waistband of his pants.

"Finished with her?" The Vagabond Killer narrowed his eyes. "You said you didn't know her. Who is she to you?"

"No one," Mark said. "You're paranoid."

"You're lying. I can see it. I can see the devil light in your eyes." Without further provocation, the Vagabond Killer lunged at Mark, his knife extended. Mark caught the man's wrist and the two were locked together in a struggle.

Carey had a chance to escape. A split second later, she raced in the direction of the burning house, the smell of burnt wood and ashes carrying to her nose.

Her foot caught in a hole and she stumbled to the ground, the frozen earth biting into her hands. She heard her name shouted from behind. She looked over her shoulder at the shadow moving closer. The Vagabond Killer was coming for her.

Reilly's shoulder felt as if it had been half-cleaved off his body. The acrid smell of smoke hung thick in the air and despite his blurred vision and foggy mind, the situation came rushing back to him. The house was on fire. He'd been shot. Someone—Mark or the Vagabond Killer—had taken Carey. A man's voice threatening her was the last thing he remembered. How long had he been out? Was he too late? It was still dark. How much time had passed?

He had to help her. Nauseated and exhausted, Reilly reached for the strength to spur his body. Save Carey. Protect her. He dragged himself to his feet. The gun he'd had in his hand was gone, but the other was tucked against his back, pressing into his spine. He drew it out and mentally thanked his father for teaching him to carry backup.

He refused to think he was too late. The path in the snow led behind the barn. Struggling to remain conscious and ignoring the black spots that dotted his vision, Reilly followed the tracks.

He'd asked Carey to trust him. He'd promised he would keep her safe. All he needed was one good shot and the man was dead. He had to protect the woman he loved.

Love. He loved Carey. Maybe he'd loved her all along, but now, the emotion was crystal clear to him. So obvious, he didn't know why he hadn't named it before. Reilly couldn't lose her. Not now. Not when he had plans for a future, plans to make her happy.

He focused on Carey, feeding off energy from the warmth and joy inside him at the thought of her. Letting it propel his legs and fuel his rage, he moved along the side of the barn, bracing himself against the wood.

The footprints in the snow continued around to the back of the barn. Reilly commanded his legs to keep moving as he grappled to remain conscious. A little farther to Carey. He wasn't too late. He would find her.

Checking the bullets in his weapon, Reilly put it in his good hand. If it was the last thing he did, he would keep Carey safe.

* * *

Carey fought to stand and run, but the Vagabond Killer was on her in moments, pulling her to her feet. He wrapped his arms around her, pressing her to his chest. Struggling, she tried to break free.

Another shadow appeared on the field, a familiar figure. Relief flooded her. He wasn't dead. "Reilly," she screamed. "Run, Reilly." However he had managed to get to her, he couldn't risk his life now. He wouldn't have had time to get medical treatment and was losing too much blood.

Had he heard her warning over the sound of the fire? If he'd heard, he didn't heed it. He limped in her direction and she could read pain in every step. Her heart twisted in her chest. Reilly was prepared to die to protect her.

The Vagabond Killer's breath was rank as he clutched her against him. "Ah, beautiful Haley. My angel. I took care of him. He won't come near you again."

Carey swallowed, trying not to be sick. His knife moved close to her neck. Was that blood on it? Or a shadow? Her stomach wretched violently. Mark. He had attacked and killed Mark.

Reilly lifted his gun, pointing it at them. "Don't move. Put your weapon on the ground and get your hands up."

"You can't have her. She's mine. The only woman worthy. She is an angel. She cannot be sullied with your filth."

"Drop the weapon," Reilly repeated. "I'm not going to ask you again."

"You're not going to shoot her," the Vagabond Killer said.

"Last chance," Reilly warned.

She needed to free herself enough to move and give Reilly a clear shot. "Please, Reilly, just go. John and I were meant to be together."

Confusion flickered across Reilly's face. Then he lowered his gun, his shoulders slumping.

"John, let me look at you."

His grip loosened a fraction of an inch and she leaned back. She brought her knee up and slammed it between his legs, shoving him away. He stumbled, letting out a roar of rage. He righted himself and lunged at her, the blade of his bloody knife aimed at her heart. Fear-fueled adrenaline sent her twisting away from the knife's reach.

A gunshot echoed into the night, then another.

The Vagabond Killer crumpled into the snow.

Two more men appeared on the field, racing toward them. The moonlight cast its beam and she made out their faces. Harris and Brady had arrived. Relief swept over her. Finally.

A moment later she was at Reilly's side, helping his brothers carry him to safety.

"For the hundredth time, I'm fine. It's a small sprain," Carey said, coming to her feet. Reilly had insisted she be checked out at the hospital, but it was unnecessary. "You were shot. You're the one who needs medical care."

"The doctor said to take it easy on your ankle," Reilly said. His arm was in a sling, but he refused to admit to her it hurt. It had to hurt. "And I wasn't shot. I was grazed. Harris and Brady won't let me forget I passed out from being grazed by a bullet."

Carey knew his brothers' teasing hid the fear they'd felt for Reilly. "You lost a lot of blood and I'm fine."

Reilly studied her face. "You always say you're fine.

You didn't just fall. You were kidnapped and witnessed two murders."

Actually she hadn't seen either Mark or the Vagabond Killer die. "I didn't see anything. No lineups. No witness testimony needed."

"What are you going to do now? Do you need to return home to take care of your father's affairs?"

Carey shook her head. "No, I don't want any part of the family business. I spoke to Harris while you were with the doctor. The government has confiscated my father's assets as part of an ongoing investigation. I'll be able to get back photos and sentimental things from our house, just memories. It's all I want. I have a new life now."

"You're amazing," Reilly said. "And I should have done better. I'm sorry."

She looked from Reilly to the door, sadness tightening around her heart. "You were great. Why are you apologizing? For saving my life?"

He shook his head and stepped closer, setting his hand on her cheek. "For not protecting you better. If I had been a few seconds later—"

She set her finger over his lips. "You weren't. You were right on time." They'd had this same conversation three times. Reilly's guilt was unneeded. She was fine. Honestly and truly fine. Maybe for the first time in her life. It was finally over. She didn't have to run anymore.

She set her hands on Reilly's chest. "Thank you for giving me a future."

Reilly wrapped his uninjured arm around her, anchoring her to him. His eyes connected with hers. "Tell me then, what kind of future do you want?"

The answer came strong and sure. A life with Reilly. A home. Family. "You. I want a future with you."

"Should I call you Haley?"

She could use her real name now. It sounded amazing on his lips. "Yes. Please. Haley sounds wonderful."

A smile spread across his face and happiness shone in his eyes. "I love you, Haley. I have no reason to hold back. No reason not to tell you. I love you and I want to spend my days with you. All my days and all my nights. I want to come home to you."

Her heart filled to overflowing. She blinked back tears of overwhelming happiness. "I love you, too." The words surged in her chest, filling her with bliss. Happiness. Security.

He leaned closer, rubbing his nose to hers. "Marry me, Haley."

Joy filled her chest to bursting. "Does this mean you'll cook for me?"

He lifted a brow and inclined his head. "Only if you do the laundry."

She laughed. "Guess this means I'll have to change my name again."

"Only if you want to," Reilly said, lowering his mouth and brushing his lips to hers.

She smiled against his lips. "Haley Truman? Yeah, I like the sound of that."

* * * * *

COMING NEXT MONTH from Harlequin®
Romantic Suspense
AVAILABLE SEPTEMBER 18, 2012

#1723 THE COWBOY'S CLAIM
Cowboy Café
Carla Cassidy
When Nick's secret son is kidnapped, he and Courtney,
the woman he left behind, must work together to save him.

#1724 COLTON'S RANCH REFUGE
The Coltons of Eden Falls
Beth Cornelison
Movie star Violet Chastain witnesses an Amish girl's kidnapping,
so grumpy ex-soldier Gunnar Colton is assigned to protect
her—and babysit her rambunctious toddler twins.

#1725 CAVANAUGH'S SURRENDER
Cavanaugh Justice
Marie Ferrarella
A woman finds her sister dead and goes on a rampage to find
out the truth, running headlong into romance with the
investigating detective.

#1726 FLASH OF DEATH
Code X
Cindy Dees
With a dangerous drug cartel out to kill them both, can wild child
Trent break through the cold, cautious shell Chloe has erected
and find love?

You can find more information on upcoming Harlequin®
titles, free excerpts and more at www.Harlequin.com.

REQUEST YOUR FREE BOOKS!
2 FREE NOVELS PLUS 2 FREE GIFTS!

 Harlequin®

ROMANTIC
SUSPENSE
Sparked by Danger, Fueled by Passion.

YES! Please send me 2 FREE Harlequin® Romantic Suspense novels and my 2 FREE gifts (gifts are worth about $10). After receiving them, if I don't wish to receive any more books, I can return the shipping statement marked "cancel." If I don't cancel, I will receive 4 brand-new novels every month and be billed just $4.49 per book in the U.S. or $5.24 per book in Canada. That's a saving of at least 14% off the cover price! It's quite a bargain! Shipping and handling is just 50¢ per book in the U.S. and 75¢ per book in Canada.* I understand that accepting the 2 free books and gifts places me under no obligation to buy anything. I can always return a shipment and cancel at any time. Even if I never buy another book, the two free books and gifts are mine to keep forever.

240/340 HDN FEFR

Name _____ (PLEASE PRINT) _____

Address _____ Apt. # _____

City _____ State/Prov. _____ Zip/Postal Code _____

Signature (if under 18, a parent or guardian must sign)

Mail to the **Reader Service:**

IN U.S.A.: P.O. Box 1867, Buffalo, NY 14240-1867
IN CANADA: P.O. Box 609, Fort Erie, Ontario L2A 5X3

Not valid for current subscribers to Harlequin Romantic Suspense books.

Want to try two free books from another line?
Call 1-800-873-8635 or visit www.ReaderService.com.

* Terms and prices subject to change without notice. Prices do not include applicable taxes. Sales tax applicable in N.Y. Canadian residents will be charged applicable taxes. Offer not valid in Quebec. This offer is limited to one order per household. All orders subject to credit approval. Credit or debit balances in a customer's account(s) may be offset by any other outstanding balance owed by or to the customer. Please allow 4 to 6 weeks for delivery. Offer available while quantities last.

Your Privacy—The Reader Service is committed to protecting your privacy. Our Privacy Policy is available online at www.ReaderService.com or upon request from the Reader Service.

We make a portion of our mailing list available to reputable third parties that offer products we believe may interest you. If you prefer that we not exchange your name with third parties, or if you wish to clarify or modify your communication preferences, please visit us at www.ReaderService.com/consumerschoice or write to us at Reader Service Preference Service, P.O. Box 9062, Buffalo, NY 14269. Include your complete name and address.

HRS11B

Read on for a sneak peak of
JUSTICE AT CARDWELL RANCH,
the highly anticipated sequel to
CRIME SCENE AT CARWELL RANCH,
read by over 2 million readers,
by USA TODAY *bestselling author B.J. Daniels!*

Out of the corner of her eye, she saw that the SUV was empty. Past it, near the trailhead, she glimpsed the beam of a flashlight bobbing as it headed down the trail.

The trail was wide and paved, and she found, once her eyes adjusted, that she didn't need to use her flashlight if she was careful. Enough starlight bled down through the pine boughs that she could see far enough ahead—she also knew the trail well.

There was no sign of Jordan, though. She'd reached the creek and bridge, quickly crossed it, and had started up the winding trail when she caught a glimpse of light above her on the trail.

She stopped to listen, afraid he might have heard her behind him. But there was only the sound of the creek and moan of the pines in the breeze. Somewhere in the distance, an owl hooted. She moved again, hurrying now.

Once the trail topped out, she should be able to see Jordan's light ahead of her, though she couldn't imagine what he was doing hiking to the falls tonight.

There was always a good chance of running into a moose or a wolf or, worse, this time of a year, a hungry grizzly foraging for food before hibernation.

The trail topped out. She stopped to catch her breath and listen for Jordan. Ahead she could make out the solid rock area at the base of the falls. A few more steps and she could feel the mist coming off the cascading water. From here, the trail carved a crooked path up through the pines to the top of the falls.

There was no sign of any light ahead and the only thing she could hear was the falls. Where was Jordan? She rushed on, convinced he was still ahead of her. Something rustled in the trees off to her right. A limb cracked somewhere ahead in the pines.

She stopped and drew her weapon. Someone was out there.

The report of the rifle shot felt so close it made the hair stand up on her neck. The sound ricocheted off the rock cliff and reverberated through her. Liza dived to the ground. A second shot echoed through the trees.

Weapon still drawn, she scrambled up the hill and almost tripped over the body Jordan Cardwell was standing over.

What was Jordan doing up at the falls so late at night? And is he guilty of more than just a walk in the moonlight?

Find out in the highly anticipated sequel
JUSTICE AT CARWELL RANCH
by USA TODAY *bestselling author*
B.J. Daniels.

Catch the thrill October 2, 2012.